MW01146167

ISBN-13: 978-1477537275

ISBN-10: 1477537279

LOVE NEVER ENDS

BOOK ONE OF THE FESTIVAL SERIES

Cover photo by Shawn M Knox

Back author photo by Dian Luker

Robin Lynn Wildes

Love Never Ends

Book One of the Festival Series

Dedication:

This book is dedicated to my mother, Linda Fay Wildes. Thank you for always being available to read yet another draft. You brought books to life when I was a child…here is hoping I learned well, those lessons you taught. I love you always.

Author's Note:

When I first became involved with this fictional family, it was the oldest sister, Adriana that I identified with the most. Through plotting the three sisters I saw my hero Larson as quiet, confident, but almost insignificant. Until one evening, I was having dinner with my friend Paula and we started talking about true love; how when two people are meant to be together, it just happens, and nothing can stand in its way. I started thinking of Larson then, and that is when I realized that his story was much more involved than those of his sisters. After Paula and I finished dinner, I wrote down some of those ideas. After the story took root, it was clear to me that not only did Larson's story need telling, it is significant enough to be his own book, and that this story should be first.

While Seneca and Abbeville are real towns in South Carolina, the majority of this novel is of my imagination. I hope you enjoy the first novel in the Festival Series: Larson and Margo's story.

Robin Lynn Wildes

Prologue

November 18, 1996

The tall-distinguished gentleman that exited
the sleek black limousine was noticeable immediately.
Dark-haired and wearing sunglasses, he nodded to
the two gentlemen who got out to flank him. His dark-
skinned hand held a walking stick, a gold bracelet
hung regally around his wrist. Together the three
entered the front door of the hospital. It was early.

Mornings at the busy hospital seemed to click
normally through the routines, but in the quiet wing
that held the maternity ward, there was an air of
calmness added to the routine.
The nurse on duty for the private room entered to pick
up the empty breakfast tray from the table beside the
bed.

Margo smiled, thanking her, and looked down
at the sleeping infant in her arms. Dreamily she
thought of her husband, Larson, who was due to
come collect them in just a few hours. How much this
baby looked like him, from the tuft of brown hair to the
peachy soft complexion, she was every bit a

combination of both parents. The baby curled her fingers around her mother's hand and sighed in her sleep, her bow of a mouth making sucking motions. Alexis.

Margo had made Larson go home to his parents' house early that morning, when it had been clear to her how tired he had been. He'd been with her throughout the entire birth, together, as they had been for the past two years. It had indeed been a struggle, but not so much so that with every breath she breathed a prayer of thanksgiving. Their little family was growing, little Alexis, Lexie for short, was just the beginning.

Another nurse entered the room, approaching Margo's bed slowly. "Would you like me to take the baby to the nursery, Mrs. Evans? It will give you some time to get ready for your homecoming."

Margo snuggled her baby girl close for a moment, almost unwilling to let go of her child. Then she sighed, conceding to the thought that a shower would indeed be wonderful.

The nurse gathered up the sleeping infant, secured the blanket in the classic wrapping technique used by maternity workers, and placed the baby gently in the clear plastic cubicle, rolling her out of the room.

Margo fingered the edges of the beautiful crocheted afghan that Larson's mother had made for the baby. Dreamily she thought she couldn't get much happier.

She shrugged into the robe the hospital provided and went into the bathroom to take her shower.

Fifteen minutes later she came back into the room, dressed and brushing her hair. She stopped short and gasped at the sight before her eyes.

The dark-haired gentleman sat stiffly in the rocking chair at the foot of the bed, his hand twirling the sleek cane.

"Papa!!" she exclaimed.

The man smiled, nodding toward the bed, indicating her to sit.

"We need to talk, my dear."

A foreboding fear slinked through her, dropping her stomach like a stone in a pool. Compliance and years of duty had her obliging the older man, for she knew what was to come. She noticed he held some paperwork in his hand and raised an eyebrow in question toward him.

"Your discharge papers," he answered her unspoken question. "It's time for you to come home. Your time is up."

~~~~~

Clyde Evans stirred his coffee looking into the depths as though the answers to life itself were contained therein. "A festival can be the best time of year for memories to come alive. " Outside the air was cool, and fall had settled in the small town of Abbeville, South Carolina. People were bustling around readying the streets for the *'Old South Thanksgiving and Harvest Festival';* a yearly event right out of the history books. People came in period dress, the period being 1860, and it was indeed as if people stepped back in time to carriage rides and tent camps. Clyde got into all of the pomp and circumstance, as an amateur re-enactor, carrying his rifle astride a borrowed horse with pride. His family business, 'Evans Fine Catering and Bakery' was successful and an integral part of every festival in the small southern town, and there were many.

With every event there were many more parties that kept his staff busy for days.

Now his oldest son was sitting at the table. He was supposed to be getting ready to go to the hospital to bring home his young wife and newborn daughter, but somehow the morning had him lingering at the table, with barely a dram of coffee left in his cup, listening to his father's sage advice with a grain of salt and a good measure of respect. The phone rang just as Clyde Evans had started the story of the glorious day when Larson, first-born son of the Evans clan had arrived at his own parent's house. The pride and faraway look in his father's eyes had him raising the nearly empty cup to his lips and swallowing, his own dreams and wistful thoughts in his mind while the words of his father mingled amongst his thoughts.

"Saved by the bell,' his mother, Sylvia handed him the phone. "It's for you, a Mr. Prescott?"

Larson nearly choked on his coffee, and quickly stood to get the phone his mother held out to him. The ladder backed cane chair wobbled unsteadily at the sudden movement. Sylvia calmly righted the chair, and shoved her son toward the back of the kitchen where the long cord would reach, giving him some privacy.

Mother and father exchanged amused looks.

Larson came back into the kitchen about ten minutes later laughing and picked his mother up in a bear hug, swinging her around in circles. "You are never going to believe who that was."

"Mr. Prescott?" Clyde said dryly.

Larson looked at his father blankly for a moment, and then laughed. "Yes. Mr. Prescott. He is from the law firm Prescott, Newman and Miller in Boston. They want me, Dad. I am to move to Boston in just a few weeks, with Margo and the baby. They have arranged everything! Oh just wait until I tell Margo. I will give you the details later. I have to get to the mall and pick up that car seat we ordered for Lexie. I'll see you guys at lunch time with my new little family."

Together they watched their son hurriedly swallow what was left of his coffee and leave the kitchen. "Do you reckon he'll stop to breathe before lunch? " Clyde asked his wife of twenty plus years, rising up to get a refill on his coffee, pausing by her chair.

"He's never suffocated himself before," she mused, and then the gist of what Larson had told them came clear in her mind.

Tears shimmered in her eyes when she looked at her husband. "Boston?"

"Boston," he repeated, lovingly patting her shoulder. "So," he shrugged, "we'll travel."

~~~~~

A multi-passenger golf-cart scurried its way toward the entrance of the hospital. Aboard, Larson juggled an infant car seat, a basket of cookies from the catering shop, and a large pink bunny. The wheels of the golf cart squeaked as the driver pulled to a stop next to the walkway.

"Good luck, Son," the driver said as he disembarked with the lopsided load. The bunny seemed to wave goodbye to the driver making the old man smile.

Larson made the trip to the maternity floor taking the elevator straight up. He smiled at the pretty nurse behind the counter and put the basket up in front of her. "All for you, courtesy of Evans' Fine Catering" he quipped, making his way down the hall toward his wife's room. He was nonplussed at the shocked look she had given him; he had been getting that look all morning ever since he bought the bunny at the mall. He knew that Margo was going to be giddy with excitement when she heard his news.

Not unlike the movie "The Firm", the law firm was setting him and Margo up with a luxurious fully-furnished condominium, moving expenses and a reasonable sign on bonus. All they had to do was show up after the Thanksgiving holiday. It was news that warmed Larson, but he knew that the news was not going to be a real surprise to his wife. Margo had been behind him, supporting him emotionally, from the beginning. She would always tell him that he was smart, and would someday be a big name in the legal field. Maybe even a senator or a congressional representative. She could just tell, she had said.

'Well, I can just tell too,' he thought to himself. His little family was about to be rewarded for its sacrifices of law school and doctorate degrees. Nothing in God's great world could shake his feeling of optimism.

Or so he thought.

As he reached the door to his wife's room, it was open. He imagined she was more than ready to say good-bye to hospital food. He wanted them settled in the guest room of his parents' house before lunch. However, the sight that met his eyes brought complete shock and dismay to his world. The room was empty. He quickly put the bunny and car seat on the slightly rumpled hospital bed and went to the small bathroom. Nothing. He swung open the doors of the small wardrobe, the empty hangers swayed mockingly with the movement. He walked back to the bed, and his eyes drifted across to the hand crocheted blanket his mother had given them the day before. She did not even take the blanket.

A nurse cleared her throat, making known her presence behind him.

"They left twenty minutes ago Sir, I thought you knew."

A thousand emotions flooded through his body. Where would she go without him? Or the car seat, but really *him*. A noise caught his attention and his mouth hung open in disbelief as another nurse holding a clipboard entered the room, rolling the clear bassinet with the tiny pink bundle wriggling inside. His heart began to beat loudly in his chest as the full extent of the events of the morning became clear. Alexis Evelyn Evans was still there. His wife had left him, without their daughter.

~~~~~

At his parents' house later that day, his mother sat in the old family rocking chair, cradling her first grandchild. Larson was pacing with the phone in his hand, the receiver to his ear, talking to his sister Nikki. Nikki had only graduated college last year. With his wife. She was now in grad school, with dreams of becoming a music promoter, and already had quite a few contacts with people in various places. She was also his wife's best friend. He was trying to be patient as he waited for her investigation results. Unfortunately, Nikki had nothing to report.

"What do you mean, no one's seen her?" hushed fury was barely controlled in the tone of his voice. "She just had major surgery, how far could she have gone?" There was a pause and the slight color change in her son's eyes told Sylvia an answer had come to them. "Him, yes, I didn't think of that. Okay, check that and get back to me." Softly he replaced the receiver into its cradle, instead of slamming it, as he wanted to do so badly.

"Did she say anything last night?" HIs mother murmured quietly, still gazing intently at the sleeping angel she held.

"'I love you. ' 'She is so beautiful. ' 'We will have a dozen more someday.' All the stuff she was supposed to say, I guess. Where did she go, Mom? Why didn't she take Lexie? "

The answer that popped into Sylvia's mind also came across Larson's thoughts as well. Her family. The phone, still in his hand, rang sharply.

Larson picked up the handset and shakily held it to his ear.

"Hello?" Larson listened intently to the person on the other end, his mother watching his face as it changed emotions with every word spoken. "Ok Sis, I love you too. See you Wednesday night. Bye bye"

"Well that takes all," Larson looked at his mother. "Nikki says Grenaldi's limo was at the hospital this morning. Margo must have left with him."

"But why leave the baby?"

"Yet another inconvenience in the eyes of the great Robert Grenaldi of course, like I was…like our marriage was. Anything that does not lay into the ultimate plans of the *Señor* is subject to immediate removal."

To hear her son speak so viciously about something or someone was unsettling at best. More alarming was the realization that his assertions were most likely accurate. Señor Grenaldi had been overbearing, a subject best avoided throughout the days of her daughter Nikki's stay at the University of South Carolina in Columbia. Throughout the whole wedding process, his demands had been alternately obstinate and uncaring. Still, Sylvia looked lovingly at the sleeping infant and could not understand anyone not wanting a part in the bringing up of her child, especially one so beautiful. To take an imaginary vendetta to a completely new level was something even beyond the Grenaldi reach, but she could see that it could have happened. Knowing that, she said as much to her son.

"Exactly Mom, what's done is done." He looked down surprised to be still holding the phone, and continued to pace around the living room. "Margo loves me. In her mind, she's only falling in line with some idea of loyalty. I am not concerned for her; what concerns me is what length of time she will give them?" Larson had placed the phone back onto the small table beside his mother's chair in the living room. He stopped pacing long enough to stare at the photo of him and Margo, on their honeymoon, less than a year before. It sat in a silver frame, depicting them both, laughing into the camera, their arms around each other, the spray of the ocean behind them. He smiled ruefully and nodded, as if to reassure himself of his words. "My wife loves us, she'll come home."

~~~~~

In a private plane somewhere across the state, Margo sobbed softly. Her dark hair hung around her face, the meal before her untouched. The elderly man across from her sniffed disdainfully at her turmoil.

"Tears are such a waste of time, my Dear." Robert Grenaldi said. "Now that you have come to your senses, your man will have his career, and you will live your life undaunted by menial tasks such as child care and dishwashing."

"I liked doing dishes," she said softly.

He slammed his fist on the table in front of him and in a booming voice shouted, "You will listen to me!" Margo flinched as though she had been struck, watching the emotions turn quickly from anger to calmness in a matter of seconds. "There will be no more talk of this marriage nonsense. There will be no more talk about babies, nappies, catering, and anything else you women create to make men weak. They are no longer your concern, my pet. I am. It is what I want, and I will have what I want. Do you understand?" His voice had taken on a tinge of threat, but the meaning of his words could not have been clearer. This was a promise, not a threat.

"Yes Papa," she whispered.

"Do you understand?" he repeated, leaning close to her face, "I can still call my contacts and make that wonderful new job of your husband's disappear with the wind. Do not test me. Now one more time, do you understand?"

Imagining Larson's handsome face in her mind, the sight of her little girl in his arms, a wistful but knowing look on his face, she summoned all the strength she had from the depths of her soul, and drawing on her love for them, she firmly looked into the eyes of her Grandfather and said, "Yes, Papa, I understand. I am done with them."

Robert Grenaldi sat back in his seat and turned his attention to his newspaper. Margo picked at the now cold chicken meal in front of her and gazed out the window at the lights passing beneath them. She may be through in body, but her heart would ever be with them.

Chapter One

November 8, 2012

Though it rarely stuck here in the South, Margo noticed that a light snow was fluttering in the air on the quiet streets of Seneca, a small town in South Carolina. Her hair swirled lightly around her face, causing her to toss it back over shoulder. Her smile was slight, marveling at the serenity of the scene before her.

Here among strangers, she had made her new life, where people called her by name and no one knew her past, a past she so desperately tried to forget. She stopped at the little cafe next to the antique shop across from her store. One of the sidewalk tables already held Roy and Arnold Miller, seventy-something retired teachers, twins, and local historians. They would often debate local scandals heated sometimes, then burst into good-natured laughter and buy each other lunch.

They took a moment away from their morning game of checkers to nod in Margo's direction. She stopped and smiled at them, bracing herself for their daily diatribe.

"So when you gonna get Tom Clancy in that little store of yours Margo," Roy asked her, his brown eyes twinkling with mischief.

"'Bout a month after Grisham has a number one romance on the shelves. Who could handle those kinds of crowds?"

"I'd play bouncer for you pretty lady," Arnie said, adding in his two cents worth.

This sent Roy into recanting a story about their old military days and with his attention momentarily diverted, Arnie moved his checker to the back row exclaiming, "king me," sufficiently stopping his brother's reverie.

"You cheated," Roy accused, his story forgotten, staring at the board before him in bewilderment.

Chuckling Margo left them with their banter for the different din of the busy coffee shop.

The owner of the antique shop stood in front of the large display case licking her lips sub-consciously over the pastry items. She looked up somewhat guiltily, and smiled in her direction, prompting Margo to acknowledge her.

"Morning Gail, how are you this morning?"

"Better than I deserve," she said, continuing to smile, "Hey, stop by my shop before you open, Margo, I have something you are just going to love!"

"Oh?" Margo raised an eyebrow in question toward the woman, and reached for her coffee, already fixed the way she had liked.

"Just come on by when you're done here," Gail abandoned her idea of a pastry treat and picked up the bottle of water she had set on the counter.

"Another diet Gail?"

"Another attempt at any rate. Hate to see these old friends go," she said, patting her thighs lovingly, "but a girl needs to look her best at forty." She walked out the door, the bell above jingling merrily as if to say goodbye.

Margo smiled at the thought of Gail's being anywhere near fifty. Gail was 50 if she was a day, but there was a lot to the older woman that did not add up, and Margo had never taken the time to dwell on the details. They each ran their businesses, resided in the small town and enjoyed the anonymity among the tourists. She turned her attention to the pretty attendant at the counter and added a whole wheat and carrot muffin along with her coffee. She reached forward to pay the girl behind the counter, who handed her a semi crumpled life section of the newspaper.

"I saved it for you Miss Margo, "she said, "Supposed to be a good crossword today."

"Thank you Katy," Margo smiled and turned to exit the shop. A couple of tourists came through the door looking for warmth at one of the tiny tables inside the cafe. The day had begun as usual.

An automated dinging rang when Margo opened the door to Gail's shop, "A Time Forgotten". Gail looked up from her computer and rose to greet her. She reached forward to put her coffee and bag on the counter and took her arm, leading her toward the back of the store.

"I saw this come in and just knew you'd want it. It will fit in right nicely in your little ritual I'd expect."

The *ritual* was simple. Every year for the past eight years, since she had arrived in Seneca, Margo bought a present for Lexie, the daughter that she had not seen since the day after she was born. She would give each gift to Nikki and in turn Nikki mailed them to Lexie, along with a quote from a poem or an inspirational saying. She hoped with all her heart that both Larson and Lexie knew the gifts were from her, and she knew that Lexie treasured each one. It was a way for her to stay a part of her daughter's life, even though she had not seen her since she was a day old.

Margo turned her attention to the display table on the edge of the long counter in the back of the store. On it, in a box, still full of packing paper and Styrofoam peanuts, was an ebony and silver music box in the shape of a carousel. Four brightly painted miniature horses seemed poised to dance in a circle at any moment. The whole piece was barely eight inches square. Gail took it out of the box gently and pushed a button on the base. The horses began to rise up and down, rotating in a circle, the tune "Always on My Mind" playing melodically.

"What do you think?" Gail asked, a knowing smile on her plump face.

Tears sprung to Margo's eye as she watched the tiny horses circle their silver pole, and nodded in agreement.

"Perfect," she managed. She fingered the delicate edge of the canopy to try to shrug off the unsettling display of emotion.

"I'll have it ready for you by the end of the week. We can take care of the paperwork then. Want me to wrap it like last year?"

"That's not necessary; I kind of want to take care of this one myself. Nevertheless, thank you so much for keeping such a careful eye out this year. Come over later if you want, I'm discounting those Kasey Michaels romances you like so much." Margo took a few steps backward and collected her things before turning to exit the little shop. Outside on the sidewalk she hoped she did not look as stricken as she felt. Taking a deep breath, she crossed the street to her own shop, pulling out her keys. She walked slowly willing her heart rate and her emotions to subside.

The bell above the door rang softly when Margo slipped her key into the door and unlocked her little bookshop. The cool interior met her and the silence seemed deafening. It was what met her every day. That quiet part of each morning when she reflected on the courses her life had taken. If she had not succumbed to her grandfather's wishes, where would she be? Would she and Larson have had more children? What kind of woman would her daughter have grown into if she had been a part of it? She allowed herself a few moments each day for "what ifs" then settled into her daily routine. She set her coffee on the counter in front of her shop and went to hang her coat and purse in her office. A picture of Larson and Margo taken on their weekend at Tybee Island after their marriage was on her desk. She lovingly caressed the silver plated frame that showed Margo laughing, her head thrown back, and Larson's arm around her, his face full of laughter and love. If a magic lamp came into her possession, she would gladly give up two of the mythical wishes. Her only wish was to have that weekend at the beach back, where she could have warned Larson about her grandfather. Papa had told her to enjoy her short-lived fantasy, for in a years' time she would be alone, with only her family to comfort her. Señor Grenaldi was adamant that the only source of true happiness and success was the family. His family.

If she had told Larson the extent of power and strength her grandfather possessed maybe the resulting heartache at her departure would not have been so hard felt. She knew everything that had gone on the first few weeks after she had left. She had cried continuously and begged her parents to let her return. A deep depression overtook her, so deep her parents were worried. Weeks passed, then months and she made no effort to move about or get on with her life. She just went through the motions, eating, dressing, and sleeping.

Then one morning, sitting on the veranda outside her room she saw a picture in the paper of Larson in front of the courthouse holding a press conference. He was the defense attorney for an up and coming business mogul accused of murdering his father-in-law. For weeks, Margo followed the case, on television and in the papers. She felt like she was there in the courtroom each day watching her beloved doing what he wanted. When the jury acquitted after a brief deliberation it became apparent to her that what her grandfather had done literally did provide for her young family. Larson was on a few morning talk shows, interviewed by Larry King on CNN, and it was clear that the young upstart attorney, single father to a beautiful baby girl, was someone to watch. It was then Margo made her decision to stay out of their lives, but to rid herself of her family as well. If she could not have the family she wanted, she vowed, she would have no one.

The only person from her past that she saw and spoke to regularly was Nikki. Nikki had been her college roommate. It was through Nikki that Margo had met her brother Larson. Nikki knew where she lived, visited when she could and supplied her with pictures and videos of the ever growing and maturing Lexie.

Margo shook her head to stop the flood of memories playing. The past was where it belonged, and she had work to do. She stepped quickly to the back of her shop, put on the latest CD collection from Yanni, and made a pot of chamomile tea for her reading group that was coming in around 11:00 A.M. They were to discuss a new James Patterson novel, and it was going to be hectic.

After the group broke for refreshments, and the members began to mingle and peruse the book selections Margo gave over the reins of the shop to her assistant Darcy, and went back to her office to do some paperwork. Her cell phone blinked that she had a message, and checking the missed calls realized it was her friend Nikki. She pushed the necessary buttons to retrieve the sure to be informative voice mail only to hear her friend of twenty some years say, "Call me, I've got a surprise" in a rather excited voice. Of course, Nikki was always excited about something, but since Margo never took an actual lunch hour, she figured a phone call would be just the break she needed before delving into the mountain of invoices from booksellers and agents.

"Nikki Evans Public Relations, Nikki speaking" was the cheery voice on the other end of the phone a few minutes later.

"You rang darling?"

"You actually rang back! On the same day, have you missed me?"

"Oh, you know I have, now what's up? I have 15 minutes devoted to you and your latest adventure."

"Oh really, and you are at this moment at your shop, is that right...the shop you OWN and therefore should answer to no one?"

"Let's not get snippy; you know I care a lot about my rapport with my employees. Now taking a lunch break when I could actually be working is just something I do not do, so let it go."

"Not even for your best friend, who drove all this way?"

The voice on the phone suddenly echoed and Margo looked up and saw her old friend standing in the doorway of her office, cell phone held open in her manicured hand, a sly winking smile on her face.

"What are you doing here?" she exclaimed, jumping up to hug her friend.

"I've come to take my over-worked best friend to lunch, and beg a couch to sleep on for the night as there isn't a decent place to stay in this horrible little place."

That was not true at best, but everyone knew that when any of the Evans' clan was in the general vicinity of South Carolina they stayed at the family house in Abbeville with massive rooms and old country charm. Margo said as much laughing at the thought of her mid thirty-something friend avoiding the home life for a day or two.

"Of course you can stay at my place; I'd love to have you. Lunch? Hmm," she thought for a moment and remembered a nice little place just north of the square. "Let's go to Red Wings, they have great food and it won't be busy during the day."

"Well come on then, I drove straight down from the Charlotte Airport and I'm starved."

Chapter Two

Fifteen minutes later, they were sitting in the smoking section of a small bar on the outskirts of the square. The neon beer signs illuminated a side of the room where they sat, and the waiter came quickly to get their drink orders.

"I'll have a Chardonnay," Nikki said smiling at the young man, "and my friend here will have coffee, as she never drinks anything else."

Margo looked over the menu and pretended to be interested, her mind going in several different directions. When the waiter left to get their drinks, Nikki reached across the table and tapped on the menu to get her friend's attention. "You can't fool me, you know. You are thinking what would bring me to this little slice of small town life when my life is otherwise full of exotic destinations and happenings. Am I right?"

Nikki leaned back in her seat and lit one of her customary cigarettes, pulling deep on the smoke before letting it out in a classic French inhale. Margo watched her closely her eyes narrowed then shook her head and reached out her hand.

"Still pretending to have quit I see," Nikki laughed, handing the cigarette over to her friend, and lighting another for herself. "I'm only allowing you one, so make it count and you are going to pay for it, as you are going to listen to my yearly lament, the reason I have chosen to grace you with my awesome presence."

"Lament away," Margo, said, inhaling deeply and wondering again, why such a bad habit had such a calming effect on her.

"As you know, Lexie's birthday is next week. Moreover, you know as well as I do that it is a big one. Sweet 16. Don't you think it's time you introduced yourself to your nearly grown daughter, the one you haven't stopped thinking about since the day she was born?"

"Try about six months before that, when we found out she was a she," Margo murmured.

"So not the point." Nikki continued, "More to the point is my poor, sad brother, who also has not spent a day without thinking about you and your crazy family. You could just call Lars-"

"No!" Margo exclaimed, "I could never call him. What would I even say after all this time?"

"How about something like, 'Hey handsome, remember me? I didn't really disappear off the face of the earth like you thought, and I've left that crazy demented family that held me in line and under their thumbs all my young life. I love you with all my heart, so, if you don't mind, how 'bout we get together and see if the sheets still sizzle between us?"

Margo nearly choked on the half-smoked cigarette and stubbed it out; tears streaming down her face, the waiter arrived with water and their drinks and looked at them expectantly.

"We need another minute or two doll, come back in five won't you?" Nikki smiled her devastating smile at the young man who blushed and backtracked away from them.

Nikki studied her friend closely from her perch across the table, and shook her head slowly. "You do still have it bad for him don't yah?"

"He is my other half. The reason I breathe every day. But he's on his own, and doing just fine without me, so why would I want to make waves now?"

"Speed boats make waves sweetie," Nikki said, raising her menu up again. "Love is."

Margo followed suit, pretending to study the offerings, when in reality her thoughts were in turmoil over her husband, who brought forth a question that bore answering, so Margo put the menu down again, and looked her friend squarely in the eyes. "Just what do you think my appearing after 16 years would accomplish?"

"Happiness? Fulfillment? You tell me, because I know you've thought about it."

"Of course I've thought about it, but that doesn't mean it should happen. People think about all kinds of things, living in a mansion, winning the lottery, the end to Cancer and Alzheimer's disease. Doesn't mean it will happen, or even has a chance to happen Nikki. I think I should just stay right here in the present and leave the past to the historians."

"Cop out," Nikki murmured under her breath, but turned her attention to the waiter who had appeared as if on cue. Nikki nodded to Margo who chose a Caesar Salad with marinated chicken and Nikki opted for a bowl of French Onion soup and the Mandarin chicken club.

After he left them, Margo took a sip of her coffee and sighed. She stared out at the view offered by their seat next to the window, noting the happy people strolling and milling about the area, a far-away look in her eyes as she spoke.

"You know very well I think about it all the time. However, I know it is not for the best. Not right now. I will eventually contact them, but I cannot do that while she is in such a perplexing time of her life. Now, let's table this discussion for now, and you tell me some of the antics you have been doing. I've said all I'm going to about Lexie and Larson."

Nikki knew when to push, but she also knew when not to, so she bit the inside of her lip for a moment, nodded and then took a long sip of wine, changing gears as she swallowed

"All righty then, let me tell you about the new band I found."

~~~~~

Larson was going to be late.

It was inevitable that his daughter would spend the better part of the early morning fixing her hair when he was due in court at 10 am. He had to get her to school, stop at the office to get a forgotten file for a deposition he had that afternoon, after the judge dismissed his current case. The judge would dismiss when he saw that the flimsy evidence that the prosecution had was not going to be admissible.

Nonetheless, he had to show up, and Judge Malloy was not one you wanted to keep waiting.

Frustrated, he walked back to the stairway that entered the kitchen and called once again, "Lexie! Are you trying to make me crazy?"

The pint-sized peanut that could beat a linebacker into shape given the chance answered in a pixie like voice as she descended the stairway.

"Lighten up Dad; we've got oodles of time!"

"Oodles," he repeated, looking at his watch a third time, shaking his head. "Four years of private school in New York and 'oodles' is the best narrative you can come up with?"

Lexie giggled and gracefully browsed by the refrigerator, pausing to take out a yogurt and a string cheese package. She sat down on a stool in front of the marble counter-top in the dining area and fiddled with the plastic cheese covering. "Begging your pardon dear Father," she said, in a slightly exaggerated, proper English accent, "but you needn't worry about the time. We have an extensive amount before us."

Larson looked at his daughter with a raised eyebrow, his hair suddenly in his eyes. For a split second, he saw Margo, and his heart lurched inside.

So much like her mother, he thought to himself, and she would probably never know it. He shook off the unwanted emotional burst and handed her a spoon.

"Snap to it regardless"

In the car a scant ten minutes later, Lexie started bombarding him with questions about when she could start driving.

'Driving?' A small, startling clutch of fear sprang into Larson's throat making him nearly choke on the wheat and honey bagel he had most recently consumed. When it seemed like only yesterday that they had moved to Boston, Larson could hardly believe that that little girl that clung to his hand on the first day of school; ran into his arms when he'd pick her up from camp; bowed with her face beaming at her first recital at the tender age of 6; this little girl of his memory was talking about *driving*!?? Her voice snuck back through his head, interrupting his wistful memories, forcing him to pay attention.

"I have a chance to take Driver's Ed in school next semester; you just have to sign my slip. I'll *be* sixteen!"

"We'll see Sweetie," he said, his patent answer for conversations he was not ready to have with her. "Now do you need anything for after school?"

"Well, Courtney, Alissa and I are walking to the mall after track, so some money would be nice. Oh, and can you get Nigel to pick us up at the mall around six?"

Larson nodded as he pulled into the circular drive of the magnificent high school where her friends waited excitedly. He put the car in park and pulled his wallet from inside his jacket. He pulled out a fifty, thought for a moment, and pulled out his personal bank card as well, handing them both to her. "Keep it under $500.00 please," he quipped, smiling when she leaned across for a hug. Slim, athletic, the picture of grace and beauty, she was every bit her mother. It did not seem to matter that her friends were waiting. She always said 'I love you,' and kissed him before they parted for the day.

"Want to do something special for dinner tonight?" Larson swallowed past the lump in his throat, forcing his lips into a smile.

"Food!" she laughed and kissed him on the cheek.

He watched her with a wistful smile. He looked at the dashboard clock and relaxed when he realized he would not be late after all.

He enjoyed the drive into the city. The four-lane highway did not seem to be as clogged with traffic as he made his way across the Mystic Tobin Bridge into the Back Bay area of Boston. Just outside the park, across from the famed Boston Commons, Larson pulled his Lexus into the multi car parking structure that had once been a bus station. Private parking now for the financial and business commuters of Boston, the structure sat adjacent to the John Hancock building, a huge glass structure so magnificent it seemed to end in the Heavens themselves. It was near the top of this beautiful building that his law offices called home. The lobby was like a small city, a few restaurants, a museum, a gift shop and gallery, elevators and an escalator. There was always some artist or another displaying their paintings or sculptures in the wings of the great tiled floors. People milled busily along the esplanade as though in perfect mesh to a symphony played in the background. If you stood on the balcony of one the office suites in the top, and watched, it looked just that way. It was a happy and safe existence for someone who was successfully driven. For Larson, it only fueled his career, the only part of him aside from his daughter that was alive. Any romantic wishes, feelings or thoughts remained dormant as they had since the day his love, his true love, left him. She was in his heart, long since buried, but nonetheless there. Around him, women watched him, smiled, flirted and tried to gain his attention but none of them were of any interest to him. No one could claim that piece of his heart. He did not even bother to look.

He went about his business daily without knowledge of the real world. All that existed for him was Lexie, and his career. He had, with help from a small staff, managed to combine fatherhood with a successful law career. He had money, fame, prestige, and a happy teenager to show for his hard work. He was successful in every way that mattered, and that was all that concerned him. He knew he was a good-looking man. He was not naive about that, nor that he had become a virtual Poster Boy of the law world. Every magazine from New York to LA wanted to do articles about him, the successful "bachelor". He was actually still legally married. He could never bring himself to file the papers that he had prepared so long ago. His heart was not ready to let go of a woman who gave him up so easily. So easily, that she simply walked away. For sixteen years, she had been gone, but the one thing that held him bound to her was the fanciful notion that those mysterious gifts were from her. Anyone that would take the time to purchase, prepare, wrap and send the perfect gift every year had compassion. Even, admittedly, love. They may be anonymous, but both he and Lexie felt they were from her. Well, Lexie knew, Larson just hoped. Lexie had since stopped sharing the gifts with him, somehow sensing his heart's lurch as he studied the packaging for a sign of where she was. His heart, his love, was somewhere, and that kept him going when the loneliness got the better of him.

Chapter Three

Five O'clock traffic in down town Boston was not the place for Larson to realize his cell phone was running low on battery. Successful lawyer, in a thousand dollar suit with a blinking light on his Blackberry, yep, he was the picture of success. He ducked into the small bar on the corner of Boylston Street and Tremont, and scanned the slightly growing crowd. His boss, Benjamin Prescott was sitting at a small table on the side, a half glass of *Chivas* in front of him. It was always *Chivas* in the early afternoon, Martini's at lunch, Espresso at morning meetings and Cognac in the evenings after a bottle of whatever wine was appropriate. Larson limited his drink to neat Scotch, and only one, after the workday. One. Benjamin noticed his junior partner's entry and signaled for the waiter to bring him his drink. Larson sat down across from his boss and turned off his phone before it made its hideous cry for recharging.

"You wished to see me Sir?" Larson loosened his tie and shrugged out of his suit jacket before he sat down.

"I've got a present for you Larson." Benjamin said, pausing as the waiter but the Scotch in front of him.

"Will there be anything else for you sir?"

Prescott dismissed the waiter with a wave of his hand, which had Larson leaning forward to catch the name-tag on his vest, made a mental note, planning to put a few extra dollars on his card for a tip. I

"You were saying Sir?"

"Now Larson, we've known each other 16 years and there's no sense in dragging that SIR around when it just weighs you down and ages me. Call me Ben because I have got the case of the century for you."

They were always the case of the century to Benjamin Prescott, as his firm was the firm for the big names. Ever since that first case that Larson had handled, and won, Prescott Newman and Miller had clients from all lifestyles. From Hollywood to Washington, and every area in between, the people flocked to them when there was no hope anywhere else.

"So who are we creating a miracle for this time?" Larson asked, taking a small sip of the whiskey in front of him.

"Scott Chambers," Benjamin replied, his eyes watching Larson's for recognition.

"The Scarsdale accountant? From that Research and Development firm we're handling?"

"The same", Benjamin Prescott loved to draw out a story. While effective on a jury in courtroom, it irritated his junior lawyer who had a daughter at home.

"So what happened?"

"The Boston PD arrested him this morning at his house."

"For what?"

"Murder," he replied simply, and finished his drink. He slid an inch thick file folder across the table toward Larson and patted him on the shoulder as he stood up.

"Work your miracle boy, Scott won't do well in jail, I've already got Dennis getting him released on an OR Bond with our name behind it. Mr. Chambers should be free tomorrow afternoon for a sit-down with his attorney, and **THAT**, would be you."

With that, the older man left, and Larson sat looking begrudgingly at the thick folder in front of him.

So much for an early evening, he thought and reached for the take out menu.

~~~~~

Lexie was unimpressed by the money and privilege that her father's position with the law firm gave, most of the time. However, when she was tired after practice or laden down with packages from the mall, the car and driver, Nigel, was one of her favorite benefits. Nigel was a tall thin man of European decent, his accent thick and rich, she assumed from South Africa, as he talked about World Cup Soccer as much as her friends at school talked about the College Bowl and the Drafts. He was always in the mood to talk, and the music he listened to was always something unique and extraordinary, as though every moment of his life had to have background music. Her father did not require Nigel to wear a uniform, in fact, discouraged it, wanting her to feel as normal as a teenager could despite being driven in a classy car everywhere her father did not take her. Nigel usually did however wear the chauffeur's cap, pulled slightly down in front to hide his eyes. He was leaning against the sleek black hired car when Lexie and her friends exited the mall at precisely 6p.m.

"Did you have great success Miss?" he inquired, opening the back door for her, Courtney and Alissa, fellow members of the track team, as well as the spring tennis club, and Lexie's best friends' since grade school.

"As always, when the new movies come out, the bargains on the old ones are everywhere."

Nigel nodded, and taking the bags from her and her friends, deposited them into the trunk of the car. He then secured the doors and walked around eying everything around them.

What Lexie didn't know, Nigel was not only their driver, but also he was ex-Secret Service, as well as a Navy Seal. He had technical skills that would rival even the most sensitive computer geek, but hid it all inside a somewhat calm facade. Nigel was not one to anger; he could be lethal. However, he played the part of chauffeur to appease his boss, and longtime friend Larson, and act as a body guard to them both. After Larson had gained such notoriety from his first successful case, Nigel had been by their side, silent and ever watchful.

"Will your friends be joining us for dinner Miss?"

"Not tonight, Nig. It's going to be just me and Dad, his work and my homework." He smiled knowingly and started the car, keeping a watchful eye on the cars surrounding him.

After dropping the other girls at their homes, Nigel brought her to the homestead, insuring that she arrived safely, and that there were people at the house to be with her while he made the trek back into the city for the evening.

"Evening Bridgette," Lexie called to the woman who was putting the final changes on the table.

"Evening Miss, your dad is bringing home take out from Jacob Wyrths this evening."

"Steak Fries?" Lexie looked at the petite brown-haired woman with hopeful eyes.

"Most likely, and onion rings knowing your dad. He got a new case today so he'll have to work most of the night."

"As I have a term paper due the day before Thanksgiving break, I've got "work" tonight too…so … alas …the price one pays for being so intelligent, right Brig?"

While Bridgette did set things right in the home, she was also a personal assistant to both Lexie and Larson. She most likely had a crush on the master of the house, but that, Lexie knew, would never see light nor gain nourishment. The man was ultimately and completely oblivious to the female species.

While either most nights Larson brought home dinner, or they ate out, the table was always set with cups and dishes to accommodate any meal. That little bit of a homey feeling made Lexie sometimes wonder again about her mom. Her dad never said as much, but she knew it was always on his mind. Some digging on the internet found her name and background but nothing from the time she was born until now. It was as though she had vanished the moment Lexie had been born. Lexie took an apple from the bowl on the counter and made her way to her room. Clicking a button on the remote on her bed, her stereo system filled the room with the beginning strains of a piece from *Yanni*. She loved the way the strings and piano seemed to fly together across the air, sending her floating and soaring across an endless sky to a world altogether different. She loved music. She loved sports and classic movies, but she did not take anything for granted. Some people in her position would be snobbish, but Lexie just enjoyed life. She sat up for a moment, and glanced at the clock beside her bed. She had time before her dad would appear, she decided, and stood and knelt beside the bed. Underneath, behind a sleeping bag was a dark wooden box. Her Aunt Nikki had secretly given it to her one Christmas a few years back now, telling her that the small box had been her mother's. Aunt Nikki had been roommates with her mom in college, and had still had a few things of hers. Inside the box were several cards and pieces of stationary and a picture of her mother when she had been around 19. Lexie took it out first and studied it. The hair was the same. Her mom was standing in a tennis outfit, her racket slung over her shoulder, a dark haired man beside her. Nikki had told her it was her grandfather. While Nikki explained a great deal, nobody but her mom could explain the look in her eyes in that photo. Sadness.

Her dreams lay in that box. Her main dream was that she would someday meet the sad woman that was in that photo. Her mother. For also in that box was a note, or card to go with the various trinkets that scattered their way around her room. Every note, every card had been signed with an M. She knew that they had to be from her mother. She had first started receiving the gifts about 8 years before. The first on came on her eighth birthday. A young princess next to a unicorn in a snow globe. The quote was from Ralph Waldo Emerson, "Make the most of yourself, for that is all there is of you." She hid the gifts among her things in her room; a leather bound journal with her name engraved on the front was under her pillow. Inside the front cover another quote by Emerson, in what could only be her mother's handwriting. She only wrote special things, during her birthday week in it. She wanted to have it for a long time. Behind her Shakespeare collection was a First Edition copy of the Wizard of Oz, her 9th birthday. A glorious music box in the shape of a mountain that played, "Climb Every Mountain" and even had a miniature Sister Maria twirling on the top sat on the top shelf of her closet.

She studied the various notes then, skimming over each quickly, looking for one in particular. At last, she found it; "don't let anyone steal your dream. It is your dream, not theirs. ~Dan Zadra."

Each quote, with the exception of the journal was kept in the special box she kept hidden underneath her bed. The only thing she kept out in the open was the beautiful antique globe. Hidden inside the globe itself was a velvet lined bowl with a small painting of an Indian woman, seated on the ground, the expansive mountains behind her, her arms raised toward the sky in thankfulness and praise. It was the gift she had gotten last year, so it was her favorite. At least until the next one arrived.

At first when they came, she had showed her father. However, seeing the look of sadness had been too much for Lexie so after a while she only showed Nikki or Nigel. They always came on her birthday, so she was due to get one. She could hardly wait but it was not out of greed or selfishness that she looked forward to the ritual. It was because from the moment it arrived, and for a few days beyond, it was as though she had a mom. It made her feel warm, and even more loved than she did every other moment in her life. Silly, perhaps, but nonetheless, loved.

~~~~~

Larson stepped out of his car, laden with the bag of take out and his brief case as well as his jacket, which he just did not feel like putting back on now that he was home. He walked up the cobbled steps into the Tudor building where he had made his home since he had brought his daughter to Boston so many years ago. He smiled at the lack of leaves, the green spruce adorning the side lawn, the weepy willow tree that sat in the corner in the front. In the evenings, when twilight was just starting to make its

way across the neighborhood, he liked to imagine her
there. He remembered when he would come to visit
on weekends. He would always find her in the
courtyard outside her dorm, sitting on a blanket,
reading a book. It was why he put that bench at the
base of the tree. If only she could be here with them.
He could even see her, sitting on that bench, just
under that tree; her dark hair lifting away from her face
from a breeze, a book across her lap, the pages lightly
lifted by her hand. She had always been reading
something.

"Yoo hoo...Dad...Chowtime?"

He looked up from his daydream to see his
daughter hanging halfway out her window, an
eyebrow cocked and angled at him.

Caught, he thought, chagrined.

He nodded his head and smiled up to her.
"Yes...as a matter of fact...I thought you'd like to
come help me! It's getting cold!"

"Of course," Lexie laughed, nodding toward
the tree. "Is your imaginary friend going to join us?"
Lexie's laugh echoed from inside her room, her head
disappearing from the window.

He scowled then, not wanting to relate his
thoughts to his too young, but too wise for her years,

daughter, who at present was barreling down the steps to grab the bags from him. He forced a smile onto his face as he relinquished his hold on the take out order.

"Table is already set Dad, let's eat then we can discuss our day."

He followed her in silence, depositing his coat and his briefcase just inside the office area he had set up in the front room off the foyer.

She sat at the table, her foot swinging easily to some beat in her head, munching on steak fries, watching his face intently as he related points of his day. As to the new case he had, he just said it was going to be tough, and let it go. He would never discuss the details of any case with his child or his wife had she been with him, it was not ethical. However, he could relate crazy happenings in traffic, jokes he heard, or the craziness of the day with all the comings and goings of the various people in downtown Boston.

He finished his water, and looked intently at his daughter and asked, "Have you given any thought as to what you'd like for your birthday?"

Lexie smiled, a knowing smile, and said softly, "Yes, but I know it's' too much to ask, especially now with your new case and everything."

"What do you want Princess?" Larson asked.

"I want to spend Thanksgiving with Gram and Gramps. I want to see the festival this year."

"Oh," was all Larson could say. The beginning of a case was tough at best, but a murder trial. Well it was only a few days travel, and they could fly in and out... perhaps if the hearings were not going to be until early December, perhaps he could do it. He looked at her and smiled. "I'll see what I can do."

Later that evening in the den, he studied the file and the police reports. His assistant had already arranged bail, so he would have a meeting with Scott in his office the next day. It seems that the wiry little CPA was up to his eyeballs in circumstantial evidence. A reasonable doubt defense was possible, if not for one small detail. There was a missing piece of the puzzle. No alibi. Scott says he was in his office. The security people say they have no record and the tapes were mysteriously missing. It sounded a lot like foul play. Scott couldn't kill a spider without spending his life in confession, so the thought of the little guy bludgeoning a buxom blond with a weapon and leaving her in a pool of blood in her office…well….it didn't jive. A quick phone call to his investigator a few moments later, and the ball was set in motion. If there were something out there to find, Doug Dawson would find it. Larson took out a legal pad from his desk and started preparing the list of questions he had for his new client, starting with who his friends were, and weren't as the case may be.

Chapter Four

Margo awoke the two mornings later, staring at the ceiling, wondering what sort of medieval chanting music wafted its way into her room across the scent of woodsy incense. 'Oh Lord what Eastern Culture had Nikki adopted now' crossed her mind as she stumbled out of bed, glancing at the clock on the bedside table. Margo looked again and stared in disbelief, as the tiny hands of the wind up clock pointed to 5:15 am.

Shrugging into a robe and quietly opening the door, Margo walked into the living room of her small apartment and tried desperately to control the sudden giggle that formed its way into her throat. In the middle of the floor, surrounded by the throw pillows from her couches and loveseat, among three burning candles with incense sticking out of each chunk of wax, sat her friend Nikki. She sat coiled into a position that looked painful, her eyes closed, and her hands were outward and open, the music chanted around her. She sensed Margo's presence (or finally heard her friend's chuckle) and opened an eye. "5 more minutes" she said in an almost melodic voice and closed her eyes, continuing the rhythmic sway to the music.

Margo shook her head and wandered into the kitchen, praying there would be no goat milk or cheese curds waiting for her. As long as it did not interfere with her coffee, nobody would get hurt. She made the movements slight and concise and had a pot of coffee on to brew in less than three minutes, the comforting strains of the grinding and popping the machine made filling her kitchen, nearly as loud as the chanting coming from the living room.

The music ended and Nikki pulled herself up to a standing position. Margo watched with her mouth slightly open, at the fluidness of the motion.

"I bet the guys just melt at your feet with that one move," Margo murmured, bringing a laugh from Nikki.

"Now that you mention it," she said, smiling, her eyes dancing with mischief, leaning down to get a small green towel and mopped her face and neck.

"So, what are our plans today?"

"I don't know about you, but I have a book signing at the shop."

"Anyone I know?"

"Well it's not Mick Jagger or Alan McCartney so I don't know..."

Nikki gave Margo a playful swat with the hand towel from across her neck. "Paul McCartney," Nikki corrected, "and I do read more than your basic music bio you know". Nikki took the coffee cup offered and sat on the stool in front of the counter.

Margo patted her hand indulgently, "Of course you do sweetie" and turned to pour her own.

"Well today we have Johnathan Parker, who did a lovely write up in the Sunday Circular introducing Richard Andrews, the seacoast writer from North Carolina.

"I've heard of him," Nikki said, taunting, "He writes those sniffle books like Nicholas Sparks. People are always leaving them on the planes. I have lugged several to Momma's. She loves that sort."

Everyone knew Nikki's mom, Sylvia Evans was a closet romantic. She loved to read and design and her artwork, the paintings, the quilts, were staples in every family household. From the time the children were born, they had little reminders that they were involved in a legacy of sorts. The Evans Clan was Southern true, but their roots lay in the old country of Ireland, where you could not ever be sure if the pixie light in the woman's eyes was happiness or annoyance.

That realization came into Margo's head as she decided to stop chiding her friend. "Okay, so what would you like to do?"

"I can help you with that package...we should get it in the mail in case Lars decides to come home for Lexie's birthday."

"Good idea, you remember what I told you? It's in the shop across from mine and I think Gail has my name already on it. Check and see if it's ready today. That will save some grief."

"Consider it already done then...oh and speaking of Lexie," Nikki began, lithely jumping down from the stool and half running half hopping she went to the corner of the living room where she had stowed her bag the night before. She rummaged for a few moments then straightened with a CD case in her hand. Reaching forward she handed the case to Margo and smiled.

"Lexie's tennis matches from the Playoffs last summer. I know it takes me forever, but I do finally get some things done."

Margo looked at the plain case with the DVD inside and smiled. "Well I know what we're doing tonight," she laughed. "But don't let it take that long to send off Lexie's present."

~~~~~

Nikki loved doing errands.

She was jogging lightly across the street toward the little antique shop, not against traffic, but rather in spite of it. No cars seemed to care if people stepped out in front, it was as though the world stopped and life just existed in the sweet little town her friend lived.

The musical announcement sounded a bit tinny for her taste, but quaint nonetheless. Nikki marched up to the counter and raised an eyebrow toward the skinny red head that sat on the stool behind, earphones in her ears, gum snapping. This certainly was not the owner of the store.

"Excuse me" she said to headphones girl, who nodded and snapped her gum a few more times.

"I can hear yah," she said, "What do you need?"

"I'm here for a friend. Margo? She is buying something from Gail?"

"Right," said the girl, and got up from her spot on the stool and walked toward the back.

She returned a few moments later with the box, with the wrapping paper and tissue just still inside. She seemed to pause for a moment perplexed at what she should do next. Nikki could not stand it.

"How much is it?" she asked the gum snapper, reaching in her back pocket for her credit card.

"The price tag says one-hundred and fifty, but there's no slip inside other than Margo's name on the box...I'm not sure what to do"

Nikki bit her lip to stop herself from snapping at the girl, and presented her with her card, "Let me just pay you and I'll handle the wrapping and everything myself."

"Okay, I guess the receipt will be enough then," the girl said, taking Nikki's card.

A few minutes later Nikki was back out the door with the box, shaking her head as if to get the cobwebs out. Her disdain for the current teenage mentality almost foreshadowing her happy outlook. That would never do.

Later that evening, armed with snacks and a bottle of wine, Margo and Nikki watched the video of Lexie's game. Twice. She watched it once straight through to see the game and her daughter's athletic performance. Another time she watched it to indulge the inner strains of a proud mother's heart.

The way Lexie mugged for the camera, the graceful way she walked across the courts taking her spot to serve or receive. She especially enjoyed the parts where Lexie took the camera and turned it toward the photographer. Larson. Twice Margo stopped the DVD to get a refill of wine. Each time the screen stalled with Larson's face in the midst of a grin, or a smile, or an outright laugh. The third time Margo hit the remote however, with Larson's face mid speak, Nikki spoke up.

"You are so busted," she said, slightly slurring her words, glass in hand. "I know now, beyond a shadow of a doubt that you still have it bad for my brother." She took the bottle up from the little table and poured the remainder in her glass. "The question is," Nikki pointed her finger unsteadily toward Margo, "What are you going to do about it?"

Margo looked at Nikki, somewhat chagrined, but wistful.

"Watch it again?" she said hopefully.

"Bullshit-..You know... you can fool everybody else in this little corner of hell you have been living in for the past eight years, but not me. And don't think I didn't notice that the song from that little 'present' for Lexie was the same song y'all danced to at your wedding! You are about as over my brother as rain is dry. I love you Margo, but this has gone on long enough. This year... you tell him, or so help me, come New Year's... I will!" With that, she went to pass out on the couch, a light snore coming from her lips.

Nikki, bless her, seldom drank too much, and never felt the effects when she did overindulge. However, unlike many people, she spoke with her heart, and most directly, when she was under the influence. People around her had to either take it on the chin, or walk away. Margo was in her own house, so she had to bear the words and maybe even reflect on them at some point. First, she would finish watching the video, because, damn it, he did look good! She was entitled to drool over her husband, even if it was a film version.

Gail was rummaging in the back room and making some awful noises when Margo stopped by the next morning. She hastily put down her pocketbook on the little table beside the cash register and made her way following the noises. She stopped short of the door to the storage area, her mouth agape at the sight of her. Gail was covered in sweat, her hair hanging in strands around her plump face. There were boxes upended and spilled everywhere as though someone had ransacked the room like one of those scenes from a detective novel. The look on Gail's face concerned her. Fear. "What on earth happened, Gail? Can I help?"

Gail seemed surprised to have an audience and let out a little gasp. A light of recognition came into her eyes. "That music box...the one I said would be ready for you today. Have you seen it?"

"Gail, my friend Nikki picked it up yesterday and sent it." Margo looked around at the mess and could not believe that a little musical carousel would have caused that much trouble. "You should have a receipt in yesterday's tally."

"It wasn't logged correctly" Gail said sharply, "My investors are going to have a field day. As for that simp I hired, well she's done. I cannot afford to have my books in question. Whatever," she looked up with a surprised look in her eyes, as if forgetting the whole exchange before, and impatiently asked, "Do you need something? I have a lot to do today, Margo. "

The contrast between the woman she had known for years and the one standing before her was staggering. She did not know what Gail had gotten herself into, but it had made her brash and rude. Margo decided she did not want to have any part of it so she just made a small excuse of needing to check something, backing out of the room quickly. Gail didn't even seem to notice, but was still mumbling to herself while Margo left the shop, puzzled.

She made a call to Nikki as soon as she got outside, confirming that she had sent the gift. It was Nikki that had helped to choose this year's quotation, which was:

"Nobody can make you feel inferior without your consent."--Eleanor Roosevelt.

Margo wistfully thought back over her childhood, and sighed. It was a blessing that Nikki had come into her life. All through her childhood she had been told when, how and what to do, and she had done so dutifully.

Coming from a family rich in Irish-Italian values, the Grenaldis were more expected to be loyal to the family. This expectation was un-negotiable.

The family house in Savannah was only massive if you were unaware of the Kennedy-esque compound on Cape Cod.

While Margo had been an only child, she was not a silver-spooned debutante as were the other girls in her class. Oh sure, she had the debut ball at age sixteen, summers at the house in Savannah, private lessons for tennis and horseback riding as well as hours of time spent on the vast grounds of the main home in Massachusetts. Throughout her growing years she felt there was something missing, even though she seemingly had 'everything'. It wasn't until what her grand-father had called her rebellious stage that she discovered what it was that had been missing all her life.

Love.

Her first rebellious act had been to accept a scholarship for Literature at the University of South Carolina, rather than the expected Liberal Arts program at Amherst College.

Her second act was turning down her grand-father's offer of off-campus housing and opted instead for the coed dorm in the middle of the campus, complete with mystery room-mate.

Her father, dubbed the outsider by her grand-parents, drove her up from Savannah at the end of that summer, tearfully leaving her off at the dorm with nothing more than a hug and a credit card in her name.

The first thing she'd done after unpacking was to set up her little coffee pot on the table beside her desk. The grinding and popping of the small machine lent calm to her even then. The first few strains of home-sickness washed over her, almost having her reach for the phone to call her mother, one never to embellish the truth, but always seemed to give off love nonetheless.

It was then that her room-mate bounded through the door. Pixie dark hair, cropped short and yet becoming, her dark eyes dancing and darting here and there, assessing her surroundings. She was dressed in a white tank top, blue shorts and black spikey heeled sandals, and she was loaded down with two boxes. Behind her two gangly boys stood carrying suitcases, garment bags and what she would discover later was an electric typewriter.

"Is that coffee?" She'd asked, indicating the nearly full glass decanter.

Margo nodded, not sure about this pint-sized fireball in front of her.

Nikki had dropped her boxes on the unmade bed on the other side of the room and crossed quickly, her hand outstretched. "I'm Nikki, and if you share that, you are my new best friend!"

Their friendship was solidified over fresh home-made cannoli and the rich coffee sweetened with plantation sugar, something Nikki had never heard of, but loved instantly.

It was a friendship so strong that even that little thing of Margo breaking her brother's heart hadn't severed their bond.

A full day was over at five that evening, and there were invoices to be tallied, receipts to log, inventory to research, even cups to wash as she'd sent her assistant home after the 3 o clock book club had disbanded. Margo knew she had a lot of work still to do, but rather opted to sit in one of the comfortable chairs in the salon area of her shop, sip a cup of tea, and just listen to the sounds of the evening begin.

As she sat, her mind wandered again to the past. There were so many wasted moments. Of course, she knew Nikki was right. However, that did not stop the fear that would lodge its way into her chest every time even the thought of contacting him entered her mind. Calling would not be right anyway. No, it would be better in person. On the other hand, would it? They had always had a rather volatile chemistry, tempered with passion and a genuine fondness of each other. They had begun dating in college, and at first, even her family did not mind. However as they saw the stars appear and the light ignite between their daughter and the kid from the south, it was clear they had no use for him. Margo, or Marguerite as they called her, defied their rules and doctrines when she and Larson planned a wedding complete with a small honeymoon right after their graduation from the University of South Carolina. Larson was graduating with his law degree, taking six months to study for the bar exam, interning at a firm in nearby Spartanburg. They wanted to begin their life together.

To be fair, her mother had been supportive, and her father even agreed to the small service, and gave them a small honeymoon. It was her grandfather that had caused trouble, calling Larson a red-necked ambulance chaser. Then, all at once, he stopped his tirades, and even had a few meetings with the caterers and Larson's mother. It should have been a warning, but Margo was too in love to realize the deviousness of her grandfather's control and power.

She rose up from the chair, a tear escaping. She had not seen any of her family for over ten years. She did not even know if they were alive. When she cut her ties, she severed them, and burned the bridges that led back. If she was to live out the remainder of her life alone, then she would do so. She felt a true forgiveness for their falling to the wishes of an angry old man. However, she did not have to forget.

Chapter Five

The morning of Lexie's 16th birthday was cloudy, but rather warm in Boston. Larson had been up since 5 am putting the final changes on a report to the DA for a delay of trial for Scott Chambers. There was more evidence, and his investigator had uncovered just enough to stall the proceedings for a few weeks. Long enough to take Lexie to South Carolina, he grinned, glancing over at the airline tickets wrapped up in Hannah Montana birthday paper, an inside joke between them.

Lexie came running down the stairs two at a time, and sprung lithely upon the stool at the counter.

"Gifts" she said, smiling… knowing there would be one for now, and more at her party at the Country Club in Lexington that night.

"This?" Larson asked, holding up the bright colored paper with the kids' logo.

"You've lost it, right? I will NEVER forgive you for singing 'Achy Breaky Heart' last year! I was mortified!"

"No you weren't… and I was good"

"Well, I won't ever have a Karaoke themed party again, I assure you," she giggled, knowing that that also was a lie. She loved to hear her father sing. He was awesome, almost like a rock star if you did not think about it too much. He had been a singer in school, and still fooled around with the piano and an ancient acoustic guitar he must have had when he was twelve.

"Dang, I'll have to cancel that then" he teased, handing her the present. She opened it carefully and squealed with delight at the sight of just the corner.

"We're going? For Thanksgiving? You are so the BEST dad EVER" she jumped off the stool and launched herself into his arms.

He settled her on his lap, hugging her, and said, "Nothing but the best for my sweet 16 girl," but felt her stiffen and draw back.

"Are you sure you can get away?"

He looked in her brown eyes, and the lump in his throat threatened to break free to tears. She just looked so much like Margo, and it seemed was growing up with her heart as well.

"Yes my Darling," he said, squeezing her one more time before letting her get off his lap. "That's why Nigel will be taking you to school; I have to go to the office early. We will leave Friday and be there for a full 10 days. We will be there through Thanksgiving and the Festival. How does that sound?"

"You're the best, Daddy," she said, meaning it, "have a great day and I'll see you tonight", and ran upstairs to get ready for school.

Larson looked outside and saw the car sitting in the driveway. He waved at Nigel, and took his keys and briefcase up from the counter and headed for the door at the back. He went into the garage, started the car and was on his way to work.

Lexie came down a few minutes later and grabbed a muffin and a banana. She checked her schedule on the refrigerator, no practice, just party. She opened the front door to go to the car and saw the box on the steps.

"Time, Nigel?"

"Plenty," he smiled, nodding at her to go ahead and open the awaited gift.

Lexie picked up the box, brought it inside, and put it on the side table. She opened the envelope taped to the top first, and pulled out the familiar stationary and a small envelope. The card was one of roses and a hummingbird, with a poem about bringing art and love into your life. The card held a familiar quote of Eleanor Roosevelt. "No one can make you feel inferior without your permission". The neatly written words struck her, care given to each individual letter. It was from *her*.

She opened the box carefully, wanting to draw out the moment for as long as she could. Nestled inside the tissue paper and bubble wrap was a beautiful chestnut music box. She lifted it carefully out of the box and placed it on the table. Once out of the box she saw it was a carousel. Four beautifully painted horses sat with silver poles and ribbons. It was heavy, so it had to be musical as well, and Lexie searched quickly for any sort of on/off switch. There in front she found a little button, which she pushed and then stood mesmerized as the little painted horses started to rise up and down, and the base began to turn. The music was familiar, but she could not place it. She would have to research it when she got home though; she had a test first period. She could not afford to be late. She fingered the edge of the wooden box lovingly, then grabbed her book bag again and ran out the door to the waiting car.

~~~~~

Doug Dawson took pride in his work. He had graduated from the University of Massachusetts with a degree in Journalism, but three years at the Boston Globe had turned him off mass media. He loved digging into the truth, but hated hearing the facts distorted to make a buck, so he took a few tests and became a detective with an investigator's license. He still had plenty of ties from the paper he could rely on, as well as some of the cops on the Boston PD force. Detectives did not talk to newspapermen, but they talked to fellow detectives more freely. Doug made a habit of frequenting a little diner off Tremont where most of the foot patrol took lunch. He could eat his clam chowder and glean information at the same time, for a minimal amount of money. He sat in his friend Larson's outer office, silently watching Larson's secretary field phone calls, and waited. The news he had heard needed a personal touch. Poor old Scott Chambers had been in the wrong place at the wrong time. The similarities of the two cases, the civil lawsuit of the Research and Development Company, and the murder of Dawn Petrocelli were too much to be a coincidence. It had taken Doug about a half day to prove out his hunch. He was going to make his friend's day.

Larson came into the office and smiled at his assistant. "Any messages Abby?" he asked, his hand out for the several she seemed to always have ready for him.

"Only one you need to concern yourself with," she put the reference slips in his hand. "The restaurant called and wanted to confirm the time for your daughter's party this evening."

"Excellent!" Larson smiled, and looked toward the corner where Doug sat. "Doug, come on back, this will just take a minute."

Doug entered the plush office and walked over to the counter next to the restroom. He opened the little refrigerator, took out a Coke, snapped off the cap, and took a swig. Larson went to his desk, stowed his briefcase on the floor beside his chair and sat, reaching for the phone. Abby buzzed the office intercom. "Rafael's on line 2 Boss," she said. Larson punched the button with his left hand and held the phone to his ear, then thought about it, and just clicked the speaker button. The receptionist on the other end confirmed a guest list of twelve at 7:00 with a carriage ready to take them through Boston Public Gardens at 8:30. The Swan Boats were no longer visible, but the atmosphere in the park was always welcoming, and it was one of Lexie's favorite parts of living in Boston.

Larson ended the call and gave his friend a long look.

"Those things will kill you someday," he said nonchalantly, indicating the soft drink.

"Die trying, that's my motto." Doug quipped, and took another long drink of the popular soda. "Sounds like the party of a lifetime," Doug commented, nodding toward the phone.

"You only turn sixteen once," Larson shrugged, a wistful smile on his face. He leveled his full attention to his friend and smiled, "So, I take it you have some news?" Larson asked, pointing to a chair in front of his desk.

Doug sank himself into the rich Italian leather and paused for effect.

"What would you think if I told you Mr. Chambers had indicated to one of your other workers here that he had some interesting information concerning a few falsified tests made late last year?"

"I'd think somebody was gaining some insurance for themselves."

"That's what I thought, until I went to a few other people and found out some other interesting facts. Would you like to hear some of these never before heard facts Larson?"

"Of course, just hang on a second." Larson hit the intercom button and when Abby's voice came across the speakers he said, "Hold all calls except for Ben okay?"

"You got it"

"Continue," Larson gestured to Doug, and went to get him a bottle of spring water from the cabinet and poured it over ice. The clinking of ice in a glass always seemed to help him think.

"Well, the Research and Development firm, Scarsdale's, are an outfit out of Maine. Their main branch is in Bangor, but their corporate offices are right here in Boston. It says so on most of the letterhead. Right?"

"Yes, I have a few copies of some of that, I've been doing a bit of help for the team on that case in my, ha-ha, spare time."

"Right, so do you have any idea what that address is?"

Larson took a moment to pull the file from his briefcase, paged through a few forms and gave out the address, "1254 Dorchester Street, Suite 219."

"Care to hazard a guess as to what is at 1254 Dorchester Street?"

"I'm waiting," Doug was obviously another person that liked to draw out a good story, but they went way back, and he was good, so Larson bit back the impatience and motioned for him to continue.

"'Mailboxes ETC'. 219 is a rental box for a -" Doug looked at his notes as if for reference, and then continued. "Barry Petrocelli, the husband of our recently deceased marketing tech, Dawn Petrocelli."

"Interesting," Larson's brain started thinking up several scenarios as to why a major Research and Development firm would have a dummy office in Boston, but Doug wasn't finished with his report.

"It also seems that the main branch in Bangor has recently filed a chapter 11 suit in the national bankruptcy court in Washington."

Now this was interesting news. When a major company filed bankruptcy in the midst of a court proceeding, it usually meant they thought they would lose, so there would be no money should the other side win. Scott had just given some valuable insight on rigged tests, which brought two questions to mind. He voiced the first aloud.

"So what did Dawn *do* in her office on Tremont, if their corporate offices were at a rent a box place?"

"I thought you'd ask. Therefore, I did. It seems that Ms. Petrocelli was the courier for the mailbox place. I showed her picture to the clerk and they said she was in five or six times a week, picking up packages and mailing them out." He reached into his black notebook carrier and pulled out a list of addresses. "Here's a list of the places she mailed things off to, it seems a lot of stuff went out to only three separate addresses in the last 6 months."

Larson took the paper from Doug and looked at the addresses. Interesting enough, there was one in a town not forty something miles from his family home. A town called Seneca SC.

"I'm going to be in SC over Thanksgiving. I can investigate this one on my own. Seems Research and Design shouldn't be sending out samples of anything…if you get my meaning."

"I thought the same thing, but then again you're the lawyer, so you make the big bucks for those thoughts. I just go dig up stuff."

For Larson, Doug was a lot more than just the digger; he was a friend, and an instrumental part of his success. The cunning detective before him aided half of the cases in which Larson found himself stranded. Larson decided to go for broke and asked the other question weighing on his mind.

"Any idea what Scott did with this so called proof?"

"Funny you should ask. It seems there was a download of some interesting files off his computer, and then erased. The little geek put the files somewhere, probably a flash-drive, and erased all evidence thereof. The hackers at Boston PD cannot find a thing other than the date the files disappeared. The day before he was arrested."

Larson made note of yet another question he would have to ask Mr. Chambers at their meeting that afternoon.

Larson stood to shake hands with Doug and gestured toward the door. "Once again you have proven invaluable to me," he began, but Doug just smiled and waved him off. "Stop by Abby's desk and pick up a check, and we'll have lunch sometime before I leave."

"Lars, I'm just doing my job, but I really hope you can get to the bottom of this. It just does not sit

right with me. Mousy Scott bludgeoning someone?
Seriously!"

Larson watched his friend leave and sat back
in his chair, studying the address before him.
Something about that town jogged a feeling, and he
did not know quite what it was.

Larson had been studying the notes in front of
him when Abby buzzed him announcing Scott
Chambers was there. Time to meet the mouse, he
thought whimsically.

When people give someone a nickname, it
comes from various reasons. A bad haircut, or a
particular speech impediment, a funny name, a hobby,
a talent. Any number of things can contribute to a
nickname, and sometimes it does not even fit at first
glance. "Spike" may have outgrown his bad haircut,
"Skeeter" could have hit a growth spurt, and "Tank"
could have lost that extra fifty pounds after graduation.

At first glance however, Scott Chambers was
every bit a "Mouse". From his simple haircut, black
framed glasses, and bowtie to his wing tipped loafers
and black socks, the accountant looked like his nose
would twitch any minute. He was timid, alert, and
probably scared out of his gourd. Who could blame
him, thought Larson as he ushered the timid little man

into his office and rang Abby to bring in a service of tea. The thought of this little man spending the next 30 years behind bars would be scary to anyone. It was a matter of life and death, but the man looked as though he would pass out before he had a chance to answer even one question.

Larson took the time to calm down his client before diving into the questions he had assembled. They talked small talk for a few minutes then after the tea was brought, along with some lemon wafers that Abby had stashed somewhere, Larson got down to business.

"Scott, I know you told the police what you knew, but I need to hear it for myself. Start from the beginning."

"What beginning?"

"What do you mean?"

"Well, there's the beginning, meaning the night Dawn was killed, and there's the beginning of when I decided that Scarsdale was going to kill me if I didn't get away from them. Which beginning do you want?"

"I'll take Scarsdale for now, and we'll work our way up to Dawn Petrocelli."

Larson flipped over to a clean page on his legal pad, and gestured with his hand. Scott took a sip of tea, a bite of a cookie, and then started.

"I've been the accountant for Scarsdale Research and Development for about sixteen years now. When Alan Scarsdale retired four years ago, his son Reginald took over. Reggie was a piece of work, let me tell you, but hey, my job was the number cruncher right. What did it matter to me where the numbers came from? Then, as it always happens, the numbers started to change. Accounts had too much money in them, then not enough. Shipments started going out, and we did not have any product. We are a research firm. We have testing labs and papers published in medical journals. FDC licensing and that sort of thing. However, there they were, shipping and receiving. I had to ask what was going on. There was no place in my system for the records. When I asked about the new accounts Reggie said, 'just put it under donations, kid, and don't worry about it.' I grew up in the Back Bay Mr. Evans; 'don't worry about it' is code for shut up and stop asking questions. My uncle worked for the Sicilians, I'm not stupid."

"So what did you do?"

"I created the donations account as a secondary, and kept a record of it. An invisible one, just under the other accounts, so that only I could see the activity there. Otherwise, all the monthly finances and expenses were okay. I can pull off the geek mode very well, I have an IQ of 189, but in this business, it is healthier to be naïve and stupid.

"Dawn started calling me about a month ago. She was having problems collecting her paycheck from Reggie. I told her I was an accounting executive, not a payroll clerk, but that did not sit with her. She told me she knew I knew more, and that she would find a way to make me look bad. Blackmailing now? That was the last straw. Every time I went to Reggie with a question he said, "You're the money geek. You straighten it out" so I did. For three weeks, I paid her out of a miscellaneous account. Then I started downloading all that info of the accounts, the shipments, and the mysterious trips and dates, put them all on two separate flash drives, saving them in case I needed them. I even coded them with a GPS so if it's accessed I can find out where it is…just in case one falls into the wrong hands. The last night I took one last copy, then erased the memory. I left that office not intending to come back, took Dawn the last check I was ever going to pay her, and then went home to my apartment in Cambridge. The next morning I was awoken by the Boston Police Department, arrested and held for the murder of a woman I barely even knew."

"Where are the flash drives now?"

"One is in a safety deposit box in Nashua NH in my Mother's name. Mailed it the night I left. The other one I planted at Dawn's apartment or I guess it was her office. I put it inside a little merry go round music box about a week or so ago. I did not see that thing when I went that last night to give her the check. She must have moved it or something, but anyway, there is a little secret compartment under the base of the carousel. That is where I stashed the flash drive. I thought it would take the suspicions off me."

"Or it could have been what got Dawn killed. Does anyone else know about those files?"

"The files were common knowledge, that I had copies now that was not." Scott looked down at his lap, "I didn't even think that I was endangering her life by putting those files there. I feel horrible now."

"Don't," Larson, said, "At least we have something to go on. I think I can get the whole thing dismissed once I get those files. Can you get them for me? I'll make a copy for myself and you can keep the original"

"I'll get you a copy this afternoon." he said, standing then. "If it's all the same to you, I'd rather not make a big deal about it, just in case someone's watching me too now."

The two men shook hands and Larson reached forward and put his other hand on top. "Trust me Scott; I will get to the bottom of this."

Larson sat back, thought about what he had heard that morning, and shook his head. Someone had killed Dawn, framed Scott, and all over fudged numbers in a spreadsheet? There was a lot more to this story. A whole lot more.

When Larson came back from lunch, there was a package on his desk from Scott. Inside were the flash drive and a thank you note plus a check for $25,000. The retainers to be counsel for his trial, should there be one. Larson still hoped that the information on the drive would be enough to dismiss the charges, as there had to be someone else who would like to see Scott framed and Dawn removed. Reggie Scarsdale for one.

That evening, dressed in a creamy beige shift with black heels and a black cashmere wrap, Lexie was escorted by her father to her birthday party. Nigel held open the door of the limo and Lexie stepped out onto a beautiful red carpet walkway leading to the entrance of Rafael's, an upscale restaurant just across from the entrance to the Boston Public Gardens.

The doorman opened the door and bowed toward Lexie, her father just beamed with pride. They were escorted to the private room in the back which was elegantly decorated for the party. Several of Larson's co-workers, including Mr. Prescott and his wife were already seated around the large table, and each stood and clapped when they entered the brightly lit room. The attention caused Lexie to brush prettily, and Larson again thought how much she resembled his long absent wife.

There were pitchers of tea, lemonade and water with lemon and lime slices floating in it on each end of the table. Scattered along the center of the table were red and white rose petals surrounding small white votive candles, their flames dancing brightly among the fine dinnerware. Ben rose to pull out Lexie's chair, and shook hands with Larson in a warm greeting.

Lexie had known most of the people seated around her all of her life. They were almost like family, as much as her grandparents in South Carolina.

The laughter and dinging of dishes being brought to the table made her aware of how lucky she was.

After their dinner plates were cleared, coffee was served in delicate china cups, and each guest got a matching china plate and silver fork. Then a waiter came through the door carrying the most beautiful cake she had ever seen. It stood five tiers high, with black and white icing around the first two layers, the top three molded to model books. A beautiful structured sixteen stood on top, candles circled the base. Several other servers joined him and they all led the group singing 'Happy Birthday' to a very surprised Lexie.

That was not the end of the surprises. After she had made a wish and blown out the candles, the servers dispersed, and while the waiter was cutting the cake, the Maître de wheeled a cart loaded down with dozens of brightly decorated packages. Boxes wrapped with black and white paper, red and pink bags with tissue paper peeking out of the tops. It was all so amazing Lexie's face beamed with pleasure. A few tears came to the surface, and she dashed them away with the back of her hand discretely. She was only missing one thing. Her mom.

Dutifully Lexie unwrapped and enthused over each gift, especially the diamond encrusted silver tennis bracelet given by the Prescotts.

Nigel appeared at the end of the party to collect their bags, his eyes glittering appreciatively at all the gifts.

Lexie thanked the guests with grace, smiling and nodding with every hug until her father came beside her holding their coats. He led her outside where parked by the curb was an elegant carriage resembling Cinderella's coach, led by a beautiful white horse.

"What's all this, Daddy?"

"This is my, 'I'll be too busy in the next week to spend any time so let's take a ride and have some special Father/Daughter time' present."

She launched herself into his arms and held him close for a moment, both somewhat overcome with emotion.

"I love you more than my life," he said softly, drawing back to look into her eyes. "Now let's take a ride through your favorite place!" The driver took his place beside the door and assisted Larson getting Lexie settled on the bench, a warm blanket across their laps. Then he climbed up to his seat just behind the horse and with a snap of the reins they were off on their ride.

Full of lush trees and trails, benches and statues, the Boston Public Garden was indeed Lexie's favorite place. People came from all over the world to see the tribute to the story 'Make Way For Ducklings,' the delightful children's story about Mr. and Mrs. Mallard and their eight ducklings, Jack, Kack, Lack, Mack, Nack, Ouack, Pack, and Quack, and their adventures as they parade through Boston to their home in the Public Garden. Mrs. Mallard and her ducklings lived forever in bronze at the far end of the park.

A large elm tree with bright lights surrounding it stood as if on guard and the horse clopped along the path at an unhurried pace.

Lexie leaned her head against Larson's shoulder and sighed. "Tell me about her again Daddy," she asked softly.

He knew without hesitation that she meant Margo, and though his heart ached at the thought, he did what she asked. His voice was soft as he started telling her again about the afternoon he delivered a trunk to his sister Nikki's dorm room and met her college room-mate Margo.

Larson had been taking a short break from his studies at The University of Georgia, Law School, and he had drawn the short straw to deliver the trunk full of costumes that Nikki had forgotten the week before. "So I walked in the room carrying Aunt Nikki's trunk and there she was, standing on a chair stretching to hang a poster of William Shakespeare's 'Romeo and Juliet', the classic Franco Zeffirelli movie."

"You scared her," she remembered.

"Yes, but I didn't mean to. The door was open, it was a Saturday after all, and that's common in dorms. So, in I walk, and I startled her so badly, she lost her footing. I never moved so fast. Dropped that trunk right in the floor and caught her just as she was about to fall."

"You saved her."

Larson hesitated for a moment, and smiled. "She saved me."

He pulled her a little closer to keep her warm in the chilly November air and smiled at the memories flooding through his brain.

"She was a literary major, in her final year. I was finishing my last year of law school. I married her right after graduation and she was so beautiful walking down the aisle toward me on your grandfather's arm.

We danced our first dance to 'Always On My Mind', you know the country song? I'll never forget the way it felt when we were dancing that dance. Like we were the only people in the room."

He turned his head slightly and looked into her eyes. "I think I will always love your mother, Lexie. I guess she really is always on my mind."

~~~~~

They shared the rest of the ride in silence, each pondering the memories his words had brought to life.

Lexie never tired of hearing the story. She knew now that that little music box carousel was almost the clearest sign she could have asked for when she made her birthday wish. Her parents were most certainly still in love. She again thought she should share the newest gift, if only to ease the silent torment her father seemed to suffer even though neither his words nor his voice ever betrayed the sadness that his eyes always seemed to hold.

Chapter Six

After a week of preparation, the hearing pertaining to the case of Commonwealth of Massachusetts vs. Scott Chambers was on the judge's calendar. Lawyer and client had sat in the breezy conference room day after day, going over the information from the flash drive, as well as the reports Doug had gotten from his contacts at the police department. Smartly Scott had not said anything. It could work in his favor at the hearing, casting a wide web of suspicion on others. The police department would re-open the case. That would not drop the charges necessarily, but it would give them a better chance at an acquittal.

On Tuesday morning, all packed and ready, Larson and Lexie put their things in the car and headed for the airport. Lexie had packed the little music box, as she wanted to show it to her grandmother and Nikki.

She thought again of the story he had recounted, the dance at their wedding. The romantic in Lexie could close her eyes and see her parents, her mother in her wedding gown, her father handsome in his tuxedo, dancing slowly and staring into each other's eyes. Maybe birthdays and Christmas was for wishes, but she made one anyway for Thanksgiving. 'Please let my mom and dad find each other again,' she prayed silently. That would give everyone something for which to be thankful.

~~~~~

Gail was gone. Her shop was dark, and had been since Monday, when the last of the orders came into the shop. Margo and Darcy spent the remainder of the weekend assembling displays and setting up corners for the after thanksgiving sales. There were festivals, football games, homecoming dances and all sorts of other holiday themed events coordinated around them, and the pair had been too busy to notice.

Now, standing at the front window on Tuesday morning, she could see that not only was Gail's shop closed on a holiday weekday, but the lights were completely off. Margo mentioned it to Darcy.

"I hadn't heard of her leaving. Shoot, she'd never leave this time of year. She loved the profit too much! No offense, of course,"

"None taken," Margo said, her thoughts far away and troubled. She sipped her tea and took a few minutes, trying to remember if Gail had any family or friends around. Outside of their work, watering her plants one time when she'd been called away on an overseas buying trip, and the occasional shared lunch at the coffee shop, Margo had no idea what Gail's personal life was like. She didn't even know for sure what her last name was. While the worry about Gail was there, there wasn't time to dwell on it. The tourists had begun to fill up the store, and her book club would be meeting in less than an hour.

That's why she loved holidays. So much to do, so little time.

At five O Clock, it was time to close. There was still no sign of Gail, and it was becoming alarming, as everyone else in the neighborhood had passed through Margo's shop at one point or the other and asked about it. She had no information; just that no one had been there since the weekend. It worried her that it had had something to do with the music box she had bought from her. However, no, this was not LA or New York for crying out loud. She was watching too many "Law and Order" shows making everything look like a detective novel. She turned the sign around in the door and put out the lights. She wondered what Larson was doing, were they home for the holidays? She had not heard from Nikki, as she had had to sprint over to Georgia for a mini music festival before coming home again. She would pick up a paper and see what was going on around her neighborhood, for Thanksgiving, another year spent alone. Just knowing there was a possibility of Larson and Lexie being in the area made her want to hide out in her apartment anyway, but they had never come to Seneca before, so why would they start now?

~~~~~

Lexie was beside herself with excitement. They were in the air, on their way toward her grandparents. She loved the south, and the atmosphere. She bounced in her seat, talking about all the things she was planning to her father who barely listened. He sat in his seat next to her, his laptop open on the table in front of him, making notes on a pad that sat on his knee. Lexie decided there would be plenty of time to talk and plan after they landed. She pulled out a book from her bag from under the seat in front of her. "Willow Walk" was just another in the series of young summer romance written by her favorite author Richard Andrews. She

loved to read and share books that she found
intriguing. She had read all the "Twilight" books,
several of the James Patterson "Women's Murder
Club" mysteries, and loved Nicolas Sparks as well.
However, Richard Andrews wrote about the South, a
place she considered part of her heritage. She stared
out the window for a moment, watching the clouds slip
by underneath her, and then turned her attention to
her book. The flight continued silently for them both.

Two hours later the plane touched down at the
airport in Columbia. Larson had put away his laptop
and had drifted off to sleep during the flight. Lexie just
sat next to her father, content to read her book and
listen to her IPOD. It did not take long for them to be
through baggage claim and on to the rental car desk
where the car that Larson had already arranged for
was waiting just outside the terminal.

An attendant outside escorted them to a black
Escalade with tinted windows. "Way to go Dad,"
exclaimed the happy teenager beside him, bumping
him with her shoulder and winking. Larson just
chuckled and slid in the front seat adjusting the
mirrors. He wanted to be responsible as well as a
little showy. Moreover, with the fact he had to
investigate that shop in Seneca, he would probably

need the included GPS system. Nothing but the best, he mused, handing the attendant a folded bill.

The Evans clan had assembled for the holidays. The house was happy again with every member of the house, except for the middle sister Macy, who would be there the following evening with her husband and their boys. Lexie sat on a stool in the kitchen, peeling carrots for a vegetable tray. Her aunt Nikki stood across from her, getting all the juicy details of the teenager's somewhat busy life in Boston. Adriana kept wandering into the kitchen chewing on a pencil, adding to the list she had in her hand for last minute shopping for the dinner Thursday. Larson stood at the back door to the kitchen, the same spot where he had gotten that phone call from Prescott so many years before and watched, happy. So many years he spent growing up in this very room, and so many years it seemed he had spent away; yet the moment he entered it was as though he had never left. His sisters were still the same, his parents even more doting with grandchildren in their lives. It was a happy life.

His father, Clyde Evans came through the back door from outside and put a hand on his shoulder. "Son, daydreaming is for women...our job is to taste-test the pies, and watch football."

"Try it dear," Sylvia called in a lilting sweet voice, "You so much as break the crust off those pies in the back and I'll make sure you never see your precious team play...EVER"

"Woman...those are fighting words." Clyde went after his wife of forty years and Larson could only smile. Truth told there was probably a Clemson University cake somewhere at the shop for after dinner the following day. The rival game, between South Carolina State and Clemson University was as much a tradition in the Evans home as Thanksgiving. The men and women shared the ritual equally. Nikki could yell at a television louder than anyone. The food was always stupendous, and the cakes and pastries laid out among the dishes of meat and vegetables made young and old appreciate the excitement of the day. Sure routing for your favorite team was exciting, but being among family, friends and good food also had its merit.

That evening, sitting on the front porch of his family home, Larson sat in the old rocking chair, just smiling. While the calmness of the night soothed him, his mind found itself running back to their familiar haunts. No matter how many times he came back home, he always seemed to feel his wife's absence strongest at this time. They had had holidays together. He had spent some time in Hyannis with her parents, while her grand-parents had been on an extended European trip. He had no idea what a gift that time had been; his soon to be father-in-law had taken him golfing. There was a party at the country club where they had danced alongside her parents. He was lulled into believing that he was accepted.

He had been brought up to believe that people were people. No matter how successful his parent's business had gotten, they were more concerned with the hearts of the people rather than their wallets. Young and old, rich and poor, everyone was accepted into the Evans homestead. Margo had said it was he that stole her heart, but his family that had brought her home.

Throughout the last sixteen years, despite his wondering, and the first few years of steadfast investigation, he had only moments of anger over the whole abandonment situation. For the hundredth time he wondered to himself, if he saw her, after all these years...what would he do? And he knew...more than anything, that he would do everything in his power to never let her go again.

His sister Adriana, the youngest, came out of the house with a cup of coffee in each hand. Handing it to him, she sat in the matching rocking chair beside him and sighed as she settled in the chair.

"Gorgeous night," she smiled, sipping her coffee.

"Beautiful," he agreed, his wayward thoughts betraying themselves in his voice.

"Big brother, how are you doing....*really*?"

His first instinct was to play the strong big brother and role model but, for Adriana, that wasn't really an option. Nikki was smart and full of energy and Macy was a wife and mother now, but Adriana was the more serious one of his sisters. She lived in her own apartment just up from the family business, and she had known her own share of heartache, only recently breaking off her engagement to a junior partner in an accounting firm in Atlanta. Nobody knew why except that she'd had thrown away the bridal magazines and spent a good few weeks in a depression, throwing herself into her work.

He looked at her and smiled. "Really, I'm okay Addy. I just can't stop thinking about her. But the memories bring me happiness."

"Yeah, I get that," his sister said, playing with an imaginary piece of lint on her black pants. "I wonder sometimes if maybe I wasn't even in love with Brian, giving him up as quickly as I did. But, well, that's in the past now."

"Do you want him back?" Larson asked, concerned about the look in his baby sister's eyes.

Adriana was quiet for a minute, then half smiled.

"No," she said, somewhat surprised.

Before he had a chance to respond, Nikki emerged from inside the house, carrying a tray of cheese straws and pinwheels.

"Snacks?" She offered, holding the tray out for them.

Larson and Adriana looked at each other and laughed.

"Sure," Larson agreed, reaching his hand forward to grab a treat.

Nikki put the tray on the table in front of the chairs and pulled a bottle of water out of her pocket.

"Where's Lexie?" Larson asked, his mouth full.

"Mom's got her in the living room, sorting through pictures for the Sanders' Anniversary party. They've been married fifty years, and Tony and his wife dropped off about a hundred pictures they want displayed.

"That's right," Adriana said, getting up, "I need some for the cake I'm doing too. Guess I'll join them." She paused beside Larson and touched his shoulder gently. "It's not the same for you Lars...I didn't love Brian. You love Margo. It will be okay."

After Adriana went back inside, Nikki took a moment to size up the serious look on her brother's face.

"What's got you down bro? Talk to me."

"Same old thing I guess. I keep remembering back when Margo and I first started dating. I thought everything was going to be great. Especially after that holiday we had with her parents. I still have a hard time believing that she really left me for them."

"Oh Larson, she didn't leave you *for* them, she left with them. There's a difference you know. I know something about Margo's grand-father that you don't. Maybe I should tell you. Ease your mind perhaps?"

"Go ahead, but I doubt I'll understand anything any better."

Nikki leaned back in her chair.

"I too have had those memories, but I had dealings with the grand-father. I remember, during sophomore year I went home with her on Easter break. Not to the South Carolina house, but the one on the Cape.

"I felt like I was in one of those movies. The house was massive and full with lush green grass and the stables; they were huge and just full of horses. I thought, how wonderful to be able to just pick a horse and ride, you know? But Margo seemed to just take it all in stride, that is until we walked into the stable that first afternoon. She walked right up to one of the horses and introduced me."

Larson smiled. "Vincent?"

"Yes, Vincent De Milo. The most beautiful Appaloosa Stallion I'd ever seen. She was rubbing his nose and loving on him, you know? And then she told me the funniest thing. She pulled out a dog biscuit and told him she'd bring him back a pear later, and the horse just loved that biscuit! I thought that was amazing, and she smiled, this quiet little smile. She said, "He just loves these things. Our cook, Estrella makes them fresh for the dogs, and he'll just wander out of his paddock, right up to the window and help himself whenever she makes them. I guess he still does.'"

"Wanders out?" Larson said, questioning.

"That's what I mean," Nikki said, "I asked her about that, and she said the trainer would always hook a line to his bridal so he'd stay in the stall, but after he'd gone home for the day, Margo would take it off. She said she couldn't stand seeing anyone else chained up somewhere they didn't want to be. Sound familiar?"

"Wow," Larson whistled. "I never saw any of that."

"There's something else," Nikki continued. "That evening we came down for dinner. I had to borrow a dress from her closet, because the grand-father insisted people dress for dinner. The table was so elaborately decorated it looked like a State Dinner for a President or something. Margo looked so different. Her hair was styled away from her face, she had just a touch of make-up and her voice was so soft-spoken I hardly recognized her. Her grand-father was seated at the head of the table. He just looked up and smiled at me, but it was an empty smile. He paused, and it looked like he was searching for a nice word to say, but was having trouble finding one.

Obviously he found the whole 'college' experience disdainful, because he had this thoughtless look on his face when he started talking to me."

Nikki put herself back there for a moment, recanting every detail.

It wasn't just the way Margo's family acted; it was so stiff and unsettling, especially after she'd been rooming with the girl for over a year. At the house in Savannah, where her parents lived most of the time, things were relaxed and easy, there was even laughter. But here in the New England home, things were so formal. It's like even dust itself was banished from their world. Nikki found herself afraid to use the wrong fork, looking at the elaborately decorated table, and was caught off guard when the distinguished man fixed his eyes on her and spoke.

"So what are you studying, Miss Evans?"

"Business Management," Nikki replied, still fingering the silverware in front of her. "With a minor in Marketing."

"Really," he seemed surprised, "and what are you planning to do with your education?"

Forgetting herself, Nikki launched into her animated speech, the question had been asked to her several times and she had her answer memorized.

"Well, I have been in theater for quite some time. I love music, and I seem to be pretty good at it. What I plan to do is open my own production company. That way I can find and guide artists and musicians toward their own success."

"Nikki was offered the lead for a traveling summer company in Atlanta." Margo offered.

"What show?" Bethany, Margo's mother asked.

"Pirates of Pennzance," Nikki answered, "but it was only because I talk so fast."

The two girls laughed and the tension at the table eased for just a moment, but then the grandfather cleared his throat loudly and sounded the bell for dinner to begin. Dinner was a quiet affair. All attempts at conversation were abandoned after that. It was as though the whole thing was dismissed. But Nikki had never gotten an invitation back to the mansion on Cape Cod, and it was rumored that Mr. Grenaldi had even tried to get Nikki moved out of Margo's room.

"I never knew that either!" Larson said, somewhat upset by this news.

"Mr. Grenaldi really thought highly of himself. So highly in fact he tried his best to get me out of his grand-daughter's life. Unworthy working type I think he called me. I don't think you were any higher. The point is, dear Brother, Margo didn't leave you because she was done with you. She'd tried so hard to get away from that family; they must have pulled her back in using the only way they could. Using you."

"Oh I know that. I had a little taste of Senor's temper, when I announced at their country club that I was marrying Margo. But he'd stopped. I thought he'd changed his mind about me."

"Not a chance. That man just laid in wait until he knew he could do his worst. So, take heart, because I have a feeling she's feeling the same way you do. That love you shared was once in a lifetime; the kind that fairy tales are made of."

Nikki got up then and left Larson to his own, sipping the lukewarm coffee and thinking a bit better about himself. He hated it when his sister was right.

Chapter Seven

Larson awoke groggy the day after Thanksgiving, still full from the festivities. He asked Lexie if she wanted to go with him, but she had opted to spend the day with her grandmother at the cafe/catering shop downtown. Sylvia always had four or five projects going and could use an extra pair of hands. He stood at the kitchen window drinking coffee, and enjoyed the solitude. It did not last long. His younger sister Macy came through the kitchen carrying one of the twins, sitting him in the toddler chair at the table handing him a teething biscuit she had produced from her pocket. She poured herself of the staple brew and leaned against her big brother. Larson easily slung his arm around her, pulling her close, kissing the top of her head.

"How goes it, Kid?"

"Don't you just love the quiet time?" Macy quipped, while Ben squealed happily from his seat at the table. Brother and sister turned together and looked at the happy child smearing biscuit across the table in front of him.

"Don't yah just love kids," Larson smiled, draining the last of his coffee and pouring him another from the carafe.

"You miss these days, admit it," quipped Macy, taking a package of wipes from another pocket and cleaning the face of her baby.

"Oh, sure, drool and spit in every crevice of every surface reachable by five inch arms that stretch to a foot and a half. EVERY day!"

"Pooh," was Macy's comeback, but her back straightened slightly when her husband, Alan entered the room with their other son, DJ.

"Forgot one," Alan smiled, kissing his wife on the cheek, efficiently putting the boy next to his brother in another seat.

Lexie breezed in then and cooed over the happy boys, picking up a banana from the bowl of fruit on the lazy Susan always present in the middle of the table. She skipped over to give her father a morning hug and a kiss on the cheek.

"Thought you were going sight-seeing today Dad."

"That I am, and I'm taking this with me." He indicated the cup of coffee in his hand, and gave her a squeeze. He paused to pat the boys on the head and grabbed a piece of fruit from the bowl. He passed his mother in the hall on his way out the door. "Don't work her too hard, Mom, she's gets cranky when she's tired. I don't know how long this will take, so I may stay over. Would that be okay with you?"

"Of course, we don't need you around here anyway. Your father wants Lexie to assist him with his costume for the parade tomorrow. Try to be back for that won't you?"

"I'll try, but no promises. This case is too important, and I have a feeling there are some answers there in Seneca. I'll call you later if plans change."

He hugged Lexie and kissed her on the top of her head. "Be good," he warned, not expecting anything else.

Sylvia watched her son leave out the door, a bit of a spring in his step.

"Wonder what got into him," she thought, smiling at the family members filling up her kitchen. Warmed a body well, it did, when family was underfoot.

~~~~~

Margo opened the shop early Friday morning. She was not a department store, but Black Friday still saw a lot of business, and she was aiming to be a big part of it. She had tea brewed, pastry set out, a table of discount items set up in the middle of the store, and another with recent Best Seller's novels near the front. Richard Andrews was coming in again. His signing had been a big day for her the previous week, and she wanted to rely on more people coming to town just to meet the man. He was a nice fellow, friendly and nice to look at, if one cared to look. He always took a few minutes to chat with her when he came to town. This was his fourth signing in the past year. Darcy said he was sweet on her, but Margo chose not to notice.

The strings of an instrumental CD wafted through the shop over the aroma of the tea she had just finished brewing. She poured a cup and stirred absently, looking out the front window as the small town slowly came to life. Cars started pulling into the spaces around the square. A man walking a dog strolled leisurely by, pausing to peer into the unlit store across the street.

It had been a week since her run in with Gail and she could not believe that her friend had just simply vanished. There was more to the upset that Gail had shown that last day, she just felt it. There was no way that Gail would freak that much over paperwork. There had to be more to it.

The door jingled when Darcy came breezing through rattling about her latest unsuccessful date.

~~~~~

The directions that spoken mechanically through the GPS system had Larson taking the country road turns like a seasoned Southerner. He saw that Seneca was beautiful upon arrival. Small houses and old buildings lined the streets leading to the small square, in the center of town. After spending so much time in the big bustling city of Boston, he appreciated the small town life like his own hometown. Here, in Seneca, there were many shops on the square, from a small cafe, an antique store, even a shoe repair place on a corner in amongst several government buildings. The little GPS device gave the final destination signal and Larson pulled into a spot in front of the little store, "A Time Forgotten". The sun was shining in his eyes when he pulled his frame from the car. 'Here' goes nothing,' he murmured, walking toward the door. Larson pulled on the handle but was surprised to find it locked. Locked. He looked toward the sign in the window that said it was supposed to be open, along with one that advertised a sale starting that day. He stood in front of the quiet little shop and ran his fingers through his hair, a habit since he was in high school when he was frustrated. Here he was, ready to ask some questions, and there was nobody here to ask. 'Well, maybe some of the owner's neighbors would know something', he thought and started walking toward the cafe.

~~~~~

Darcy was attending to the book signing. Margo took the opportunity to meet and greet the fans that had driven in to meet Richard Andrews. She was standing at the front display window, putting a stack of his latest novel, "Forbidden Sun", on the table when she saw the black Escalade parked in front of Gail's shop. She noticed it because an SUV looked particularly out of place in the small town. Also because it was in front of her missing friend's shop. Tourists were in town, not only because of "Black Friday", but also because of her author, so she scanned the street looking for the owner, part of her knowing that they could be attending the little reading group in the back. Richard was still reading an excerpt, the women held in rapt attention. She shook her head and turned to leave the window when she saw him. He was standing outside the cafe, talking to Katie, who was pointing in the direction of her shop. The sandy hair fell in curls short on his head, looking slightly older but still the same simple smile. Her stomach flipped nervously and she all but lost her breath. Standing not ten feet away was her husband. Larson. Moreover, he was heading toward her shop.

~~~~~

Lexie took the boys, DJ and Bennie, outside to play in the front yard. She set the tiny toddlers into the sand box, and climbed in with them, enjoying the feel of the sand between her toes. She looked around the front yard with love and affection, reveling in the warm sun shining on a day in November.

Nikki walked outside and stood on the front porch, a steaming cup of coffee in her hand. Her sister Adriana had gone into town to help her parents at the catering shop, and Macy and Alan had taken a ride over to Greenwood to take in lunch and an afternoon movie. In the house were just Nikki, Lexie and the twins. It presented a perfect time to talk.

"Lexie, they're fine in there for a bit, come up and visit with me."

Lexie pulled herself to a standing position and stepped out of the sand box. The boys looked up at the movement, and then turned back to filling and dumping the cups that surrounded them. Happy babies.

Lexie climbed up two steps and turned sideways, sinking onto the concrete step and looked up at her aunt. "Girl talk?"

"Catching up anyway," Nikki smiled, sitting down on the first step slightly above her niece.

"Birthday was good?"

"Amazing," Lexie said, the light dancing in her eyes. "Dad took me on a carriage ride through the Public Gardens; we had dinner in a fancy restaurant with some of Dad's colleagues. His boss gave me a tennis bracelet. I think there were real diamonds in it! It blew me away. Oh- and I got the mystery gift *on my* birthday this time. It was incredible."

"What did you get this year?"

"I'll show you later, it's in my room. It's a music box. A carousel that plays 'Always on My Mind'. It's so small, you just wouldn't believe the details."

Lexie paused and looked out toward the boys but Nikki knew it was not babysitting on her mind. The change in the features on her face was unmistakable. Doubt and just a hint of sadness encompassed her delicate profile.

"What Honey?"

"You think it's her, don't you?"

Nikki swallowed the lump in her throat and nodded.

Lexie smiled. "I know it is, Aunt Nikki, I just know it is. In my heart, every time I look at those things, I just know my mom is out there somewhere just thinking about me. About us. It makes it, I don't know, easier I guess. Easier to do everything. I want her to be proud of me. But more than anything, I want her to come home. I'm so tired of seeing Daddy sad."

"What does Larson have to do with it?"

"You know, it's funny. Many kids at school have only one parent, through divorce mostly, but a couple of girls lost their dads in the Army. I have my dad, and every year I get something from my mom. They weren't divorced, she just left." She paused, stood up and went to take a twig away from her little cousin. She continued speaking when she sat back down on the steps. "She felt like she had to leave, Daddy told me. Now, I am sixteen and I want my Mom. I want her and Daddy to be together, so both of them can be happy. I will be going away to school in a year. What is Daddy going to do then? He can't work all the time. He needs to get on with his life."

"What makes you think he hasn't?"

Lexie splayed her fingers apart, and started counting, holding each one individually.

"He doesn't date. He has no real friends except for work people. The only time he ever smiles is when we are together. He puts all his emphasis on his job and me. That is it. Most of all, he thinks I don't know, but he has pictures. He looks at pictures of her all the time. He misses her, wants her to be there. With him. With us."

"After all this time, would it be a good thing if she came back?"

Nikki was on a fishing expedition. She wanted the proof. A truth that would set both her brother and his wife free. She waited, already knowing what her maturing and sophisticated niece was going to say.

"Aunt Nikki, it's what I've wished for, every year, since I started getting those mysterious presents. There is no amount of time that can go by that would erase the fact that my mom left so that Dad and I could have the life we have. That was the most unselfish gift anyone could ever give, and I am thankful every day for it. Now I want to meet her, thank her, and tell her the most important thing."

"What's that Sweetie?" Nikki whispered, the heartfelt emotions making it difficult for her to speak.

"That I have always loved her."

~~~~~

Larson followed the directions from the cafe worker, and walked purposefully across the street to the little bookstore. He saw a sign out front that advertised a book signing. Richard Andrews? Lexie loved his books. She had one with her on the plane coming down. A signed copy would be a great Christmas gift he thought, hoping he was not too late.

He stepped into the shop, the bell above his head jingled as he closed the door behind him. He looked around the room, searching for the owner. He would ask his question, hope for the best and then buy a few books for the rest of his stay. He caught a movement out of the corner of his eye, and saw. The *owner* was a ghost.

"Margo?"

She smiled, her hands trembling as she stepped toward him, cautiously. "Hello Larson." She swallowed nervously. "Guess you found me."

He did not think. He did not care. He just quickly closed the space between them and pulled her into his arms. He breathed a sigh of relief, and held. He was home.

Margo had wondered what would happen if they ever saw each other. She figured he would be mad, refuse to speak to her, maybe even throw things, but this; this welcoming embrace was something she barely dared to dream.

He pulled back a little and searched her eyes, unshed tears glistening in his eyes. "You're real? It's really you?"

Margo smiled, "Oh Larson, I've missed you so much. I wanted to talk to you so many times, but I was so afraid."

"Of what, my Darling?" he rubbed his thumbs along her jaw line, just staring into her eyes.

"I was so sure you hated me." Margo said simply.

"No," he whispered softly, shaking his head, "I could never hate you. I love you."

With that, he drew her face closer, and bent his head to capture her lips with his. With that simple touch of lips, the sixteen years that had separated them were gone, granting the dreams they never dared to speak aloud. They were together again.

Chapter Eight

Later that day in Margo's office, Larson sat in the chair across from his wife while she was on the phone. He took the time of her distraction to study the woman before him. The time had only intensified the features he remembered so vividly. She had developed a strength in her that leant to her stamina and took nothing away from the visible beauty. Her features were gentle, her voice strong as she spoke into the phone, giving the other party a stern warning that she expected her shipments in a timely fashion or cancel her contract altogether. Her assistant tapped lightly on the open door and waited while Margo concluded her conversation.

Margo looked up and silently questioned the young woman, her eyes holding a bit of warmth in their hazel depths.

"Mr. Andrews is ready to leave Margo; you said you wished to speak to him?"

She rose fluidly from the chair, nodding as she turned her eyes toward him. "I'll just be a moment," she said, leaving the office and him behind to stare at the desk and all the little trinkets and things on it. Not clutter, but organized and unique. The thing that caught his eye and gave him hope was the silver framed portrait of them on their honeymoon at the beach. He had the same print on his own desk in his office. He looked out the window facing the front of the store and watched as the author spoke to her. She smiled, warmly, touching his arm gently, excepting two books from him. Her arms went around him then and he hugged her. Jealousy in its' most finite form slammed into the pit of his stomach and he looked away surprised that his hands were clenched into fists. Questions he had no right to ask came flooding through his brain and he fought the urge to run out there and deck the novelist.

Margo returned, pausing to close the office door. She put the books on the desk in front of Larson. He looked up questioning, and reached for them.

"He signed them for Lexie; I heard she loved his books."

"Where on earth did you hear that?"

"I haven't been completely out of her life you know," she said gently, "I've been aware of a lot of things. About both of you"

He fought hard to remember how to breathe as the full implication of her words came into focus. All this time, and not a word, but she knew things she shouldn't. How, who, why, questions and more questions that needed answers and yet, he was afraid. Afraid that if he spoke too many, if he pushed too hard, she'd be gone again, and it would all be as if he dreamed. A dream that he had lived so many times before, where just as he was about to hold her she'd disappear in a misty cloud and leave him alone again.

Steeling himself for that possibility, he looked into her eyes and said the only thing he could think of that would not be too much of a risk.

"We need to talk," he started, and then laughed awkwardly as she had spoken the same words across from him.

She smiled and nodded, "I already cleared the afternoon with Darcy. Can you come home with me? Do you have time? I can make us something to eat. We can talk there, no distractions."

Giving her home court advantage would be another risk he was not sure he could handle. However, the thought of losing her again gave him pause to reflect that while he loved his job, his house, his life in Boston, he loved this woman before him even more, and at that moment, he would move Heaven and Earth to get his family back together.

He shakily agreed and stood, willing to follow her anywhere.

~~~~~

Margo hoped that her hands were not shaking as she drove the few short blocks back to her condominium. The surreal exchange, the embrace, the kiss, all seemed dreamlike. Yet here she was, leading the man of her dreams, her husband, to her home. The questions that piled into her already crowded and over sensitized brain were numerous. The thought of voicing even a few of them gave her pause. Still two questions seemed the most likely to be asked and answered with the least amount of risk. Why was he in Seneca and where was their daughter?

She led him into the house. Coolness enveloped them and she noticed the deafening quiet. Her living room seemed small and confining with him standing there, next to the fireplace.

"Sit," she gestured toward the sofa, her eyes glancing around at all the little things around the living room. Not messy, just things, and the collection of

DVD's on her entertainment center caught her eye. There on top, open was the DVD that Nikki had brought her of Lexie. Nervously she bit her lip, casually moving toward the television. Absently she began putting the DVD's away in the drawer underneath, hoping that the motion did not raise his suspicions. She was not quite ready to reveal who her little bird was that had given her the details of their lives.

"Would you like some tea?" she asked when she was done, and started to go into the kitchen.

"Sure," he murmured his voice soft and gentle, like velvet soothing her shattered nerves. She took a deep breath willing the tension to leave her body. She could do this. Just boil water and pour into a teapot... not that difficult to do. She busied herself filling the kettle when his voice came through her thoughts again from directly behind her.

"So, do you own this place?" he asked, leaning against the counter that separated the living room and kitchen.

Margo nodded, not trusting her voice. He was just too close, she thought.

"The store, that's yours as well?"

China cups rattled a bit in her hand. Carefully she placed them on the counter next to the stove and searched for the tea tray. Was he really making small talk, she thought, trying desperately to breath in a normal fashion, her heart hammering in her ears?

She must have spoken aloud, for she heard his voice over the roaring in her ears and the beginning sounds of the teakettle on the stove.

"I'm peppering you with questions to stop me from doing what I want to do. Have wanted to do since I walked in the door of your shop two hours ago?"

"Which is?"

She watched, holding her breath as he closed the space between them. His arms went around her and his hands brought her to him close. So close, she could hear his heart thudding in unison in a rhythm that matched her own. Slowly, just short of teasingly, he brought his head down to hers, his lips a shadow of a space apart from hers. He was giving her a chance to run, to stop the next logical step, the ultimate act on which only dreams had given her reprieve in the past years of their separation. She needed answers, she needed to know things, she wanted to know what they were doing, but she needed him more. Just as that kiss in the bookstore gave promise to her that he still cared, she answered this kiss with the passion that had lain dormant inside her for so long. She was done with questions, done with self-recrimination and reproach. Done with fear. The time was at hand to end this hungering need, and she reached up the last inch and surrendered.

He gave and she took. He increased the pressure of his mouth and she knotted her fists in his hair and pulled him closer. A moan escaped, and he couldn't tell if it was one or the other that had spoken, and he drew apart from her to study the face he still held in his hands. His life, and his beloved, lay safe in the depths of his arms. Needs that had gone unmet for so many years now came flooding to the surface and won out over all else. He drew back further; satisfaction came seeing the look of alarm spring to her eyes. He leaned forward bringing his head near her ear, reaching out one hand he turned off the burner under the teakettle with a flick of his wrist. His voice, velvet edged and strong husked against her ear, "I'm thirsty, but not for tea." Then he claimed her lips again end all thoughts ceased.

He swung her up into his arms, the last conscious thought was he was not going to love her in a kitchen, but rather make her his again in a bed. Instinctively he carried her out the doorway and down the narrow hallway, pausing at the open door of her bedroom. Claiming her lips again, he lowered her to the bed in front of the window. Unhindered by sunshine streaming in through the blinds, he reached up to unbutton the first few buttons of his shirt. She reached up, taking the job over herself, her fingers moving quickly down the column of buttons that covered him. Free at last she let her hands smooth through the fabric and touched him, making his eyes close at that gentle yet heady act. He pulled her hair loose from the clip that held it in place, and pushed his fingers through the ebony tresses. Then just as he thought his control was intact again, her lips brushed against the skin at the base of his throat. Madness true and harsh took over as he brought her body up to his and took her mouth. Just this side of violence, the pent up desire that coursed through his veins that only she could answer, won over all else.

There was no mistaking his arousal when he brought her against the length of his body. His hands divested himself and her quickly, needing that contact of skin against skin to sooth the ache that circled like fire inside him.

"So long," he whispered, lovingly as he moved his body against hers, reveling in the satin feel of her length. The sensitized tips of her breasts brushed against his chest and he closed his eyes, feeling her tremble, trembling himself. She was older, but her body still answered his as though no time had passed. "Too long," he said, putting himself between her legs, resting on his arms, hovering just above her. "Open your eyes," he urged, "Watch me come home to you." With a shudder and a stifled groan his body found rest in her, sheathing himself in her warmth, a moan of contentment brought from her as their union was made complete with a final thrust of his hips. Reveling in that completion for a moment, he realized her arms lifted, her hands holding his arms, urging him further, deeper inside her. She rose up then, meeting his glance, urging him to take her completely, to make her his own again.

The emotions spiraling in his stomach took root and moved him rhythmically, and so the dance began. Each searching for that glorious moment of fulfillment. When he had held back all he could, when he knew she was on the edge with him, he let go with a cry of her name sending her over with him. Encouraging her to take him, to take all he had to give her, only her, and finally, spent, he rested just next to her, his breathing fast and furious, his heart thudding somewhere outside his chest. Home.

She had dozed for a moment. Lying in his arms, the afternoon creeping slowly away leaving a dusky shadow over her room. His hand made caressing movements along her thigh, lovingly stroking her skin.

"Why are you here? In Seneca? Not that I'm complaining of course"

He chuckled, the sound echoing beneath her cheek, her head pillowed on his chest.

"Believe it or not, I was here on business."

"In Seneca?"

"That store across from yours, "A Time Forgotten"? The woman that owns it, I have some questions. I think that she can help a client of mine."

"Gail?"

"That's right," Larson sighed, pulling her just a little closer.

"What on earth could Gail have to do with a client in Boston? Does it have to do with her disappearance?"

Larson's hand stilled its motion and he brought her head around to look into her eyes. "What do you

mean her disappearance? How long has she been
missing?"

Chapter Nine

"So where was your father going on this 'sightseeing' trip?" Nikki asked over lemonade.

"Some little town called 'Seneca,'" Lexie answered.

Breathing suddenly became very difficult for Nikki as she realized the full impact of this little fact. Should she call Margo? Should she warn her? Should she have told her brother what she knew when he had asked her for the hundredth time the evening before? Would they see each other in such a small town? These and other partial questions wandered through Nikki's mind in a matter of just a few seconds.

"Aunt Nikki, what's wrong?"

Nikki took a deep breath, and forced a smile when she looked at her niece. "Nothing pet," she lied, "go on and show me your present."

While Lexie went inside to get the gift, Nikki threw caution to the wind and called Margo's cell, not knowing what she would say. Margo's voicemail picked up before the phone even rang, so she most likely had it turned off. She was probably doing some kind of holiday book signing, the store packed with tourists. She left a message for her to call her ASAP and clicked the phone closed just as Lexie came back outside.

"Here it is," Lexie said proudly, holding out her hand to show her. "Isn't it amazing?"

"Beautiful," Nikki convincingly gushed, acting as though she had never seen the box before.

Lexie sat on the steps and pushed the button on the side to start the music. While the horses pranced up and down on their little poles, her thumb encountered another button under the base of the box. A small drawer popped open from beneath.

"I didn't know it did that!" Lexie exclaimed, looking inside the tiny compartment.

"What's this?" she asked, pulling out the silver flash drive. "Do you think it's a message?"

Nikki thought carefully and quickly before answering her.

"Honey, it's obviously an antique. Your mom probably did not know it did that either. Probably just something a previous owner had put in there."

"Flash drives haven't been all that popular for that long Aunt Nikki" Lexie chided.

The girl had her there. Still wishing for more control of the situation that was barreling out of hand faster than a steam engine; Nikki decided to strike a bargain.

"Tell you what, we'll go out tomorrow and see what's on that together on your lap-top. Some place where we can concentrate and not be disturbed by the drool twins."

Lexie laughed and agreed, sliding the silver disc drive into Nikki's outstretched palm.

That bought her some time, she thought, putting the flash drive in the pocket of her jacket. If Margo returned her call before the opportunity to escape the family house came along, she would be sure to ask about the compartment and its contents. Another mystery would just have to wait.

~~~~~

In Margo's living room, Larson sat on the couch mindlessly chewing on a carrot. Margo had made a snack for them and they were sharing it in front of the fireplace. The afternoon had completely gotten away from them,.and it was evening. The daylight outside the window slipped away like sand in an hourglass. Each had their own fear of the time passing so quickly, there were so many things left unsaid. Not to mention the original purpose for Larson's trip to Seneca in the first place.

"I don't want to leave you" he said simply, "but I have to get to the bottom of this. I'm so afraid if I walk out that door you'll disappear and I won't see you again."

"I'm not going anywhere," Margo said quietly.

Larson looked in her eyes, seeing the resolve and admired her for all she'd been through in her life. "I have so many questions…real questions about how your life has been. However, this case, this man is on trial for murder, and what Gail knows could lend a great deal to his defense. I just don't want to fail either of you." He leaned forward to put his plate on the table and take her hand in his. "You understand that right?"

"You could let me help," Margo said. She turned slightly from her place next to him on the couch to face him. Her eyes searched his lovingly, encouragingly. "I've been a bit curious as to where Gail had gone. I know where she lives. Maybe I could help."

Larson gazed into her hopeful eyes and smiled. His dreams had come true. He could not believe that she was sitting next to him, encouraging him though her touch. However, just the mere thought of her in danger put him completely against her becoming any more involved.

"Honey, I want to say yes, but the risk..."

"Risk? I've known her a long time, Larson. I do not know what she got herself into, but I couldn't turn my back on her any more than you can forget your client. I was planning to go over there anyway tomorrow before work. Why don't we go together and see what we come up with?"

Larson silently thought it over for a moment. "How long has she been gone?"

She shrugged and looked away, reaching for her cup of tea to take a sip.

"She was there in the shop last Friday. I had gone by to ..." she paused for a moment, biting her lip. "Okay, here's the thing. I bought Lexie a gift from Gail. This year's gift. I have been getting and sending gifts since she was about eight. Since I left my family and started my business here."

A smile came slowly to his lips. He had known all along that those mysterious gifts had been from her, and said as much.

"So it was you! She showed me the first few, but then she never said anything. Every year?" he asked incredulously.

"Every year," she put the cup back down and took his hand again.

"The little notes? Did those continue as well?"

"Just quotes. This years' gift I sent Eleanor Roosevelt's quote, 'Nobody can make you feel inferior without your consent.' I put the card and the gift in the mail before Gail disappeared. When I saw her Friday she was all upset about it though, and that was unusual. Gail had picked out the piece for me herself. Nevertheless, there she was, that last Friday morning, all upset upending drawers and boxes looking for something so frantically I remember thinking she was into something shady. I'd never seen her act that way before."

"What did you get from her?"

"A music box. A music box that played "Always on My Mind," she smiled then. "You remember that song right?"

"Our first dance as husband and wife? How could I forget. You'll never know how much…" suddenly the thoughts in Larson's brain clicked backwards to the description.

"A music box? My client had hidden a flash drive in a secret compartment in a music box that disappeared shortly before his arrest. I wonder if that is what happened. That it had been shipped to Gail's store."

"Hidden?"

"There is a hidden compartment. I will call him and get a better description. Are you sure Lexie got it?"

"I'm sure," Margo sighed, looking down at their joined hands. "There's something else you should know, Larson."

Gently she pulled her hand away, rose, and walked over to the entertainment center. She pulled out a few DVD cases from a drawer and handed them to him.

Larson read the labels on the cases. Lexie School Circus…10 years old; Parade Flag Carrier, 12 years old; Braces off 14th Birthday; Tennis Championships, 15 years old. He looked up at her, questions firing through his over-worked brain simply put forth in a single word.

"How?"

"Your sister Nikki" she admitted softly. "I've been seeing your sister on a regular basis since I returned." Margo raised her eyes to look at him, her eyes glistening, tears beginning to spill over the rims. "It is important that you realize that I had to stay a part of your life somehow. Doing my grandfather's bidding was the last thing I wanted. I lost so much, missed so much. When I came back, Nikki was the first one I found. She's been the one mailing the gifts for me, from wherever she's been on her trips. "She seemed to know what he was thinking, 'why not him?', but she continued. "I was just so afraid to contact you, truthfully I'm still afraid of what Papa may do. I do not know what kind of power he can still reign in, but none of that seems important now that I have seen you again. I want to be with you if you will allow it. I want to see Lexie."

She sat beside him again, cautiously putting her hand on his arm. "You've done such a wonderful job raising her Larson. Do you think she'd want to see me?"

Images of happy family outings marched through his mind. Every trip, every adventure that he had shared with his daughter had been shared with his wife, even though he had been unaware. It was little wonder why he had never gotten over her; she had never really left them. Determination came to the forefront and he realized the play of emotions must have been showing on his face. He took a deep breath and slid his hands up over her lap to grab her hands. Pulling them up he kissed each one, slowly brushing his lips across the back then upturning them to place a light kiss on the palm.

"I can't think of anything we'd both like more," he told her, his voice husky with emotion. "I'm sure I'm not the only person that has dreamed of you returning."

She was uncertain, her anxiety palpable as again she saw that light and fire of desire darken his eyes. The tea was forgotten and their bodies bent toward each other, hungry again, knowing that even another moment would be too long to wait.

She pulled his shirt from his waistband; he unbuttoned her shirt and pulled it back, exposing her skin. His lips touched skin and ignited a passion that he had no choice but to match.

"I need you," he said simply, and pulled her to the floor.

Later, much later, the darkness outside overwhelmed the quiet confines of the room. On a bed of blankets, pillows, cushions and discarded clothing, they nestled together in the warmest of embraces.

Larson chuckled, gathering her close to him, sliding his hand along her spine in a caress. "Well that settles it," he said.

"What?"

"You have to come back to Abbeville with me," he decided. "We can check out Gail's on the way out of town, and I can call my investigator back home and get him on this as well."

"With you?"

"With me, "he repeated. "I am not losing you again, I can't. I have to go deal with my sister, but Lexie should see you. Besides," he paused, kissing her lightly on the lips, "I'm not ready to say good-bye to you. Okay?"

"Okay, "Margo searched his eyes, seeing the love and truth therein. Here it was, in front of her, the answer to a faraway wish. She leaned forward and kissed him, pulling back a breaths' space. "It seems like I've thrown caution to the winds anyway. Should we call your family to warn then?"

Larson grinned and nodded toward the clock on the mantle. "Sweetheart, it's almost midnight. While this is great news, I doubt it warrants waking up my parents. Besides, I don't want to give Nikki a head start. Not a chance. I still have to wonder about that music box though. If the flash drive is in it, and Gail was trying to retrieve it, could anyone else know about it? You said you're sure Nikki mailed it?"

"Larson, she should have gotten it on her birthday. I always made sure she of that." Margo paused and looked around, trying to remember where she had put her purse. She started to rise, but Larson held her in place.

"Let's just get a little sleep, maybe go out for breakfast. Then you can call my sister, and we can check out Gail's. I have a need to hold my wife in my arms for a while."

Margo felt the warmth spreading through her and she brazenly lifted herself from the floor.

"Hold your wife in bed then, dear," she smiled, her eyes twinkling, "We're a bit too old for the floor!" With that she took off toward her room.

"I'll show you old," he said, gathering up an afghan and running after her down the hall, the sound of their laughter echoing off the walls of the hall way.

Chapter Ten

Reggie Scarsdale started his day angry at the world. He expected loyalty, and got nothing but trouble since he started working with his sister.

'Stupid woman,' he thought, 'she never could do anything right. It was no wonder that his dad had insisted that she leave when he kicked out his mother so many years before. The only real reason he'd even involved her was that he felt sorry for her, but she was so reckless! He sat at a table in a hotel room, out of sorts, and hung-over. Looking across the table at two of his best enforcers, the cold smile on his face was calculating. He looked the men squarely in the eyes, handing them each an envelope of money, then threw a set of keys on the table.

"You're only job is to get that information. You've done well setting up the traitor, pencil pusher, but there are loose ends. You know how I hate loose ends."

"Yes Boss," they said in unison.

"I have it on good authority that the information is with this girl. Her father is that guy who's been investigating our business. Stupid lawyers. Can't just defend anymore, now they have to dig into things ..." he trailed off, not wanting to divulge too much information to simple workers. "Never mind about that, just go get that mouse, then you can collect the girl. She's not far from here. Small town, they're having a parade...should be easy to grab her. Call me when it's done...and don't let me down."

The men left in a hurry and Reggie looked down at his cell phone at the four missed calls from his sister. He'd call her back, ease her mind. By the end of the day she'd be dead, he decided. Nobody let him down or questioned his actions.

~~~~~

A leisurely breakfast was shared by the newly reunited couple. Margo watched her husband eat the spinach and mushroom omelet with gusto, his shirt was hanging open, and his hair still tussled from sleep. She sipped her coffee, wondering how many dreams did she get granted in one lifetime.

She picked up her pocketbook from the table beside the counter and pulled out her long forgotten cell phone.

The smile on her face slowly evaporated into a frown as her phone came on and she looked at the screen intently.

"What's wrong?" Concern tingeing his voice, he moved to stand beside her staring at her phone with her.

"Nikki," she said simply, holding out the phone to show him the blinking mailbox icon on her phone. "She's left me two messages, both urgent."

Alarm bells rang in her head while she paused to read the quickly worded messages. Both were similar. 'Call me ASAP,' 'something you need to know.'

She paused and then looked at him directly. "Did you tell her where you were going yesterday?"

"No, but I did tell Lexie. Do you think she might have said something?"

"Now who's over-reacting? It's not like the whole family isn't going to know soon anyway. We can be there in a couple of hours."

"You go throw some things in a suitcase. See if you can get in touch with Nikki and double check on that package. I'll call Doug and see what I can find out." He pulled her into his arms, engulfing her in his warmth, finding comfort. His eyes took on a serious light, a wary look in their depths. "We can leave as soon as you're ready to go to Gail's. This is starting to worry me. The men that framed my client are ruthless. She could be in serious danger."

Margo nodded moving toward her room, calling Nikki's phone as she walked down the hallway. No answer, she thought, frustrated, and waited for Nikki's message to finish playing before she left her a message.

"Nikki its Margo," she said, leaving a message on Nikki's voicemail. "I need to talk to you too. Call me back, I'll be waiting. Thanks Hun, love you bye."

Margo took a deep breath and let it out slowly. With shaking hands, she closed the cell phone and slipped it into her pocket. Looking around her room, she wondered how she could pack quickly and not seem that desperate. It was a dream come true. Surreal in that she hadn't ever dreamed that Larson would one day be in her house, much less so much still in love with her.

Was he still in love with her? Doubts crowded into her over stimulated mind and gave her pause just as she was opening a drawer to pull out a few sweaters. She looked at her reflection in the mirror above the dresser and smiled at the sight that met her eyes. Her hair was still a bit tousled, her cheeks rosy red, and her lips full from a night of his kisses. Love? Who knew, but she did know that his passion had matched hers. It was like the old days back in the early part of their marriage. Sternly she warned herself to stop borrowing trouble, and slammed the drawer shut with a nudge of her hip, and moved to the closet to pull out a few things from in there before heading for the bathroom. She heard the distinct sound of a cell phone from the other room and hurried to finish her packing. When Margo came out of the bedroom carrying her zippered bag, she looked around the apartment for Larson. He was standing by the counter, talking softly into the phone. He was just finishing his conversation when she approached, his free hand sliding down her arm to capture her hand in his.

"Call me as soon as your hear *anything*," he barked, his voice edged with irritation. Clicking the phone closed he looked at Margo with sad eyes.

"Doug called me back, Scott is missing too." he said simply.

Sympathy and fear warred inside her mind as she went to his arms. "We'll find them," she assured him, "We just need to get this show on the road."

They ran out of the door holding hands, each lending the other strength.

Once seated in the car, Margo started rummaging around in her purse. "A few months ago, Gail went on a buying trip, and asked me to take care of her plants." Margo told him. "I think I still have the key. Aha, here it is," Margo held up the small key ring triumphantly.

"Good thing that," Larson mused, "I don't think I can defend us if we're arrested for breaking and entering." The attempt at humor did not alleviate the knot of fear lodged in her stomach. With both Scott and Gail missing, something was definitely going on, and it did not seem to be good as it was bothering Larson as well.

~~~~~

Lexie's laptop sat on a table in the back of the family shop that morning. Adriana came by with sweet tea and shortbread, and the two sipped and munched happily until the cafe got quiet around them. Nikki pulled the flash drive from her pocket and motioned for Lexie to slide over the laptop to her side of the table. Inserting the silver disc into the USB port, she waited while the files loaded, questioning the validity of all this. Margo had still not returned her call, and she had no idea what was going on. Not knowing caused more worry than all the scenarios going through her head. The menu appeared in a box on the screen and Nikki clicked the file open quipping, "Here goes nothing."

In no time, a spreadsheet appeared with dates and names that had no meaning to Nikki on first glance. She looked closer and saw the addresses, where one in particular popped out from the screen. "A Time Forgotten" was the name of the store in Seneca. The number had the same exchange as Margo's little bookstore. There were several entries with that address, some with stars, and names associated. There were other addresses too, but there were no personal notes or files attached.

"It's just an inventory list of some kind sweetie," Nikki murmured to the crestfallen teenager next to her. "But at least we know."

"I don't know why I hoped," Lexie said in a choked voice, tears threatening her greenish blue eyes.

"Don't worry Honey, I have a feeling you'll see your mom someday." With all the information she had gotten from Lexie, and the reaction she had just seen, she had to talk to Margo soon. This girl needed her mother. Soon. Lexie unplugged the flash drive and put it into the pocket of her jean jacket. It may not have been from her mother, but it was connected. Nikki smiled knowingly and said nothing to the girl about keeping the worthless disc.

"Are you two going to go out for the festival or are you just going to hide in here all day?" Sylvia Evans admonished from her place behind the glass counter.

Lexie looked up from the computer screen and smiled sheepishly at her grandmother. "Honestly I'd forgotten all about it!"

"Don't let your grandfather hear that, he'll disown you!"

Lexie laughed and stood to walk to the window. Outside the townsfolk in their Civil War period dress were assembling around the town square. Her grandfather came in from the back room in his gray uniform, his beard closely clipped and his hat proudly upon his head.

"Who are you this year Grandpa?" Lexie asked softly, her voice held a hint of amusement at the serious look in her grandfather's face.

"Brigadier General M.L. Bonham, at your service!" he announced proudly, bowing from the waist, causing the sword attached at his hip to sway.

"Get out from behind my counter *'General'*," Grandma chided, "You'll knock over the pies."

Clyde kissed his wife on the cheek and did as told, his face taking on the look of a lecturer. "Are you familiar with Secession Hill Lexie?"

"Of course Grandpa, it was the meeting that took place between Jefferson Davis and his generals to plan the secession of South Carolina from the Union. It has long been thought of as the very beginning of the Civil War."

A tall-distinguished man entered the cafe just then, engrossed by the young girl's speech. He made quite the picture of dignity, his white hair and twinkling eyes dancing with excitement. Lexie took one look and immediately knew this was the man playing President Jefferson Davis, and greeted him accordingly.

"Good afternoon Mr. President, are you here to see the General?"

"You raised this one right, Clyde," the man said to her grandfather as the two shook hands. "Our carriage is out front. We should be lining up." He turned his attention to the women before him, Aunt Nikki and Lexie.

"Ladies?" he motioned for them to take his arm, moving toward the door. "Let's find you a good seat for the parade."

Sylvia laughed at that, and went back to slicing apples.

~~~~~

Watching the various peddlers milling around the square, Nikki and Lexie were in chairs set a block away from the cafe. Around the square booths, like tents, held all sorts of things from Native American beadwork to hand made pottery, hand sewn quilts and bonnets and period costumes that looked like they came straight out of a movie.

Nikki spied a look at her cell phone. One missed call. Her heart quickened at the number, Margo. She had taken a seat next to Lexie on the outskirts of the square. Noting the preoccupation of Lexie on the procession of the parade, she decided to return the phone call. She got up from her seat, murmuring she would be right back, and walked to the side of a restaurant on other side of the street where they were perched in chairs. Dialing quickly she waited for the call to connect, hoping she was in time to warn her friend of her brother's presence in her town. It was not as though the two of them seeing each other would be a bad thing, but she had to check in with her friend. She did not see what was happening not yards away.

~~~~~

People had been lining up a mile away at Secession Hill. The sound of bagpipes began to play and the procession began.

Nikki got up suddenly and walked away, leaving Lexie watching from her seat. Beautiful women in their hoop skirts and bonnets walked children in front of the horse drawn carriages carrying the 'visiting dignitaries'. She pulled out her phone to call her dad, wondering where he was and why he had not made it back yet. She was just about to ask Nikki when a juggler making his way along the side of the processional caught her attention. He was so out of place it caused Lexie to turn on the camera feature of her phone. She was just aiming the camera at the performer when she felt someone jostle her. Strong hands banded her arms and pulled her from her chair, causing her to drop her cell phone on the ground in front of her. It was as if all the sound was seeped from the air, and the darkness engulfed her.

~~~~~

A shriek of fear caught Nikki's attention and had her spinning her head in the direction of the sound. The bagpipes were blaring near her so the sound seemed only to alert her and had her running back to where they had been sitting. Lexie was gone. She heard the squeal of tires and saw a late model van disappear around the back road away from the square. So startled by the sound she had not ended the call and still had her cell phone in her hand. She pushed the end button and ran back toward the spot where the chairs sat empty. On the ground beside the folding chair lay Lexie's cell phone, still open. With a trembling hand, she reached down and picked it up, gasping at the image caught by the tiny camera feature. Large hands gripped the arms of her niece, a startled look stretched across her young face. Someone took Lexie.

~~~~~

The driveway that led to Gail's house seemed too long to Margo sitting next to Larson in his car. She had the borrowed keys in her hand, fingering them nervously.

"It will be okay, we'll look around, I'll get Doug back on the phone then we'll be on the way to Lexie.

It won't be long now." Larson said encouragingly, sensing the stress in his wife's tense body.

"I hope we find something. I just want all of this to be over. For you as well as for me."

"For us," he smiled, his crystal blue eyes shining with love.

Larson parked the SUV in the empty driveway in front of the expansive house. "Pretty house for a single woman," he mused, suspicious at once.

"I never thought of it that way, but you're right. She always seemed like she was a struggling business owner, but this house just doesn't fit the bill."

"It's beginning to look like Gail is in a lot deeper than just accepting packages."

Margo unlocked the door quickly and together they stepped inside the quiet home. A spacious foyer opened into a set-in salon carpeted with lush deep reds and polished wood. Ceramic vases and elegant portraits surrounded the living room. A large bookcase took up an entire wall filled with leather volumes and brass bookends. Mozart, Beethoven and Shakespeare busts adorned marble pedestals in the corners of the room. A grand piano sat in another corner and along the opposite wall of the living room was a large stacked stone fireplace with a deep marble hearth surrounding it. Above it hung a portrait of a distinguished man with a young girl in his lap, a young boy standing nearby, the children holding hands, a striking resemblance between them. Larson saw the portrait and immediately recognized the man in it. Alan Scarsdale.

"That's Reggie and Gail as children, I'd bet my house on it!"

Margo spun around with a shocked look, "What do you mean? As in the Reggie that is causing all those problems with your case? The one you suspect had something to do with your client's disappearance?"

"The same. That is Alan Scarsdale in that portrait. We have been representing his company since I went to work for Prescott! I thought you said you watered her plants for her. Didn't you notice all this?"

"Plants are in the back on the deck. I came in the back way and used the kitchen. I certainly don't remember seeing all this!"

The brass plate beneath the portrait confirmed Larson's suspicions. "Abigail, Reginald and Alan, Christmas 1979"

He began searching the closed doors off the foyer, looking for an office of some kind. "Here," he yelled to Margo, stepping into another richly decorated room filled with a desk and red leather couches and chairs. On the desk was a computer, phone and fax machine in front of a large window that faced the back yard. The answering machine sat silently, but next to it, the cordless phone was on the charger. Margo picked it up and looked at it, taking in the neatness of the room.

"It doesn't look like she left in such a hurry. There's not a thing out of place!"

"You're right there. Wherever she went, she went willingly and efficiently. Let me see that."

He took the phone from her and pushed the recent calls button to retrieve the numbers. "This is a Boston number. It appears several times, from what I can see. Let me give this to Doug. I don't think we need to see anything else."

Margo's phone beeped and she pulled it out of her pocket.

"I hate phone tag," she said, looking at the screen. "How did I miss this call?"

"Who was it?"

"Your sister." She started to return the call again when Larson's phone began to ring. "No more tag," Larson murmured and answered the call.

Chapter Eleven

With no time to waste, Nikki dialed Larson's number. He answered on the first ring. "Larson, I'm so sorry, Lexie's gone."

"What do you mean gone?"

"Gone. Disappeared. Taken from the parade that you hardly ever miss, right here in the small town we grew up in." Nikki covered her face with her hands and swung around, her eyes searching wildly praying she'd see her niece. "I walked away to get a phone call. I wasn't gone two minutes. I heard a scream and when I turned back to where we were sitting, all I saw was her chair empty and her cell phone. Where the HELL are you?"

"You wouldn't believe me if I told you," he said, "but there's no time to explain. You sit tight; we'll be there in an hour."

The phone clicked dead in her hand.

"We?" was the only question that came to mind.

~~~~~

Larson hung up the phone shakily. He looked at Margo, the fear in her eyes punching a hole in his heart. He gathered her close and held, offering comfort though his own fears had him nearly paralyzed. This was getting more and more out of hand, and he had to do something. Taking one last kiss, he stepped back and quickly dialed Doug's number.

"I was just going to call you," Doug told him, his voice rather rushed and full of tension.

"Talk to me," Larson clipped, grabbing Margo's hand for comfort.

"You know that GPS device Scott put in the flash drive? Well it has been dormant for weeks, but today, it seems to be on the move. Right down the road from your hometown, heading for the coast."

"Lexie must have found it; somebody grabbed her from Abbeville about ten minutes ago. I'm with Margo in Seneca; it will take me an hour or better to get back to Abbeville."

"Then don't go there. Where is the nearest airport to you?"

He took the phone away from his ear. "Where's the nearest airport Honey?" he asked Margo.

"Right here. In Seneca. There's a small municipal airport right off the main highway, on the other side of town."

Larson nodded and put the phone back to his ear. "Seneca, about fifteen minutes or so from where we are now."

"I've got a plane, and I'm on my way to you. We'll be there in about twenty minutes. I'll meet you there, and don't worry, we'll find her. I have already taken the liberty of getting Nigel, he is with me now… It looks like we will need his help to finish this job."

"Do you think they're together?"

"If I was able to trace that thing, no doubt Reggie and his guys could do it also. See you in a bit, Buddy. Bring the wife. There is no sense having something happen to her while we sort this mess out."

"Never planned anything else," Larson said, ending the call.

He turned to his wife taking in the shocked expression of horror on her face. "Don't worry," he told her, rubbing her hand with his fingers soothingly. "Doug and Nigel are special ops. There is no one I'd trust more with the safety of our little girl." He prayed that they were not too late to execute the plan to rescue his client and daughter. Just then, his phone rang again, and his heart stopped when he read the same number that he had seen on the caller ID registered on the screen.

"Evans, you're in over your head," the caller told him.

"Might say the same for you Reginald. Where's my daughter?"

"Safe for now, you just get that disc and its' copy to me as soon as you can and you can all go and live a happy."

"And Chambers?"

"Perhaps you can rescue him as well. Just depends on what kind of time you make I guess. I will call you with the drop point in an hour. I trust you won't let me down Evans?"

"'You'll get what's coming to you," Larson told him icily. When the line went dead Larson fought the urge to throw his phone across the room. Taking a deep breath, he ran his fingers through his hair and turned to Margo who was still looking at him intently. Time was already against them, and the stakes were high.

"We have to leave now if we're going to meet that plane," he clipped evenly. He forced a smile for her and pulled her toward the door.

~~~~~

Sitting at a table in her parent's cafe, Nikki sipped on the coffee in front of her, periodically checking the phone for missed calls. The sound of busy police officers and agents filled the room, the din just edging into her consciousness.

"What did he mean by 'we'?" she thought to herself, picking up the phone again. The blank screen seemed to mock her, and she could not help but feel anxious as her heart began to hope. Had her brother finally found Margo?

A man in a plain grey suit came up to the table, pulled out the chair across from her and sat down, pulling out a notebook.

"We need to go over your statement one more time Miss Evans,"

"No we don't. It does not matter how many times I tell you, it is not going to get you any closer to finding her. She's out there, not in my head!"

"I understand your frustration Miss, but this is an investigation, and I'm supposed to ask these questions, however redundant they may be."

Nikki sighed and took another sip of the now cold coffee. Her father came up behind her and patted her shoulder gently, reassuring her with a simple touch. No matter what happened, she still could not help but feel responsible for Lexie's abduction. The fact that the police were still around, asking questions, marring what was supposed to be a happy day just irritated her. Nikki was all about control, and feeling helpless was not something that sat well with her. She sighed and began her story again, from the beginning.

"I went out to the square with my father and his friends. We set up chairs on the corner and got ready to watch the parade. I noticed a call I had missed on my cell phone and stood up to return it but the signal was low, and the bagpipes had started playing so I really could not hear. I stepped away from Lexie to get a better signal and started to return the phone call. Then I heard Lexie scream. I turned and saw her chair was empty, and a blue van went speeding down the back street away from the square."

The agent wrote in his notebook while she spoke, nodding at times but saying nothing.

"Is that when you noticed the phone on the ground?"

"Yes, Lexie had obviously turned it on to use the camera."

The agent rose and patted Nikki's shoulder somewhat awkwardly. "Everything will be fine," he murmured, moving away from her pulling out his phone as he walked.

It had been over an hour since Lexie went missing.

~~~~~

The Oconee County Municipal Airport in Seneca was small. Larson pulled into a space near an office building and parked. Margo got out of her side of the car without hesitation, and stood by the front of the car. Larson stepped smoothly from the car, pocketing the keys after locking it. His blue eyes looked around trying to locate his friend. A blue and white Lear Jet sat on the tarmac, the engine running softly. The sleek lines of the aircraft shone brightly in the afternoon sun. A dark-skinned man walked from the office area and approached them swiftly, another blond haired man following behind.

"Talk to me Nigel," Larson greeted the man with a handshake and the two stepped away to converse.

The blond haired man introduced himself to Margo. "I'm Doug Dawson; I work with Larson on most of his cases. Let's get settled in the plane. Time is of the essence." Grasping her elbow he guided her toward the sleek aircraft.

Margo climbed aboard the plane with Doug, Larson and Nigel following close behind. The elegant interior of the airplane took Margo's breath away, a flood of memories crowding into her already over taxed brain. Margo had traveled in luxury when she was a child, but those days were long behind her. She made her way along the plush carpeting of the plane's interior taking a seat near the window. Doug sat across from her, and buckled his safety belt. Nigel took his seat next to Doug and Larson slid into the seat next to her.

Larson looked around at the richly decorated plane and smiled, fixing a sharp look at Doug, "I think I pay you too much."

Doug chuckled softly and explained. "I called in a favor. My Cessna would have gotten us there, but it is not as fast as this. This way we can strategize and I don't have to actually fly the plane."

The aircraft powered up and began the taxi to the runway. They were airborne in minutes, winging their way toward Lexie.

~~~~~

When Lexie first awoke, she was aware of a dull ache in the back of her head. She looked around at her taking note of the sparsely decorated room with only one window, covered so thickly with grime it was dark. A ceiling fan turned slowly above her and she noticed she was on an ugly brown couch. A woman sat in the corner of the room, holding a bottle of water. The smile on her face was sarcastic, and she looked at Lexie with hostile eyes.

"So, you're awake? The little princess. We finally meet face to face."

Lexie felt the chill from the woman's words slide down her spine like icy fingers. Defensive aggression made her words clipped and sharp. "And you are?"

"Gail Rogers. Gail *Scarsdale* Rogers. I'm the one that picked out all those nice presents your mother's been sending to you."

Lexie's mouth opened and then closed again quickly. "You know my mother?"

"Indeed. Coincidentally my brother knows your father. We're all like a little family aren't we?" Gail rose and walked toward Lexie, extending the water bottle to her, "Thirsty?" Gail asked, offering her the drink.

"No thank you," Lexie declined, twisting her hands together in her lap. "What are you planning to do with me?" she asked the maniacle woman in front of her.

"That depends on your father," Gail said simply, returning to her watch post in the corner of the room. "We have plenty of time for him to come through, and we'll tell him where you are when we are well on our way out of the country." She paused in her musings to reflect on the slight of build teenager sitting on the sofa. "You look a lot like your mother you know," she said simply.

Lexie brought up her head defiantly. "You say that like it's a bad thing," She commented softly, letting her brown eyes meet the hazel ones of the older woman.

"You think?" Gail took a few sips of her water and put it back on the floor next to her chair. "Growing up with so much money, nice things, it wasn't so bad was it?"

"What does that have to do with my mother?"

"My father left my mother. He threw us out of the house actually. My mother was never the same. She never let me forget that it was because of me that we were always on the verge of homelessness. It was my fault that we were always on the verge of being without. My father did not care one bit about what happened to me after I left. It is not so with your little family. Your mother has an almost obsession over both you and your father. It's sickening. Something tells me they would both walk through the literal gates of Hell to save the other, or you. That kind of misplaced loyalty makes a person weak. It was the downfall of my brother, and it will be the downfall of your precious parents too." Gail looked away wistfully and ended her tirade with one simple sentence. "'Happily Ever After' only exists in fairy tales."

Lexie straightened her back and leveled a steely stare at Gail. Then she looked away and closed her eyes, choosing to say nothing. Silently she prayed that somehow the bitter woman's words were not true.

Chapter Twelve

Larson leveled an ice-edged glare at the ringing cell phone. In front of him, Doug and Nigel were finalizing the plans. The plane was descending out of the cloud banking to begin landing preparations at the small commercial airport outside Charleston South Carolina. Doug motioned for Larson to answer the call.

"Yes," Larson spoke softly, his voice tinged with worry and apprehension.

"Game-time. Meet me at the old armory on River Street. Do not play games now. You know you have no life without this little girl."

"Let me speak to her Reginald, or I'm not meeting you anywhere."

"Absolutely," the voice agreed, pausing a moment to grant the request.

"Daddy?"

Larson's heart lurched when he heard the voice of his daughter. "Hey sweetie, I'll be there soon."

"I don't trust these guys…" Reggie cut off the girl's call.

"Teenagers never trust grown-ups 'Daddy'. You have what I need right?"

"I already told you as much. Do not waste my time. I will be there in twenty minutes. You bring my daughter."

"Oh I don't think so. I will tell you where she is after I get my information back. No cops or you will not have your precious reunion. It is a simple game, with simple rules. See you at the armory."

Larson did not bother to look at the phone's screen. He knew the call was over. He threw it into the seat across the aisle, feeling a bit better at the show of aggression.

"What does he expect to get at the armory?" Doug wanted to know.

"Both of the flash-drives. I only have the one though; the other is with Lexie, where ever that is."

Doug grinned and pointed toward Nigel who was immersed in something before him on a computer screen, headphones over his ears.

"Did he?--" Larson started to ask the question, but knew it was merely a waste time. Of course Nigel, special ops leader from Uganda had gotten a trace on the last phone call from Larson's cell phone. It was what he did.

White teeth sparkled when Nigel lifted his head. "There's an airstrip less than a few blocks from this place. We can be there in just a few minutes. We should strategize now so we can get her safely and then bring the authorities in to take care of the rest."

Within minutes the plane touched down at the tiny airport near the hide-out. Margo waited aboard with the pilot, feeling all sorts of useless.

She knew the game plan of course. It would take less than ten minutes to get to the hideout. Nigel, Doug and Larson would go get Lexie, and if he was there, Larson's missing client. She shuddered to think of how that was to be accomplished. Violence, guns and kidnapping. It was as though she'd stepped into the middle of one of Richard's novels. She closed her eyes and prayed. It was all she could do.

~~~~~

Gail's phone rang again startling Lexie from her mid slumber. She couldn't see outside. Gail spoke quickly in hushed tones, glancing toward the young girl as if to reassure herself that the hostage was still there.

"Be right back," Gail said, "Gotta check on our other guest.

She went out the door and Lexie heard the swift click of the lock on the other side of the door. Locked in, windows were probably nailed shut. How was she going to get out of here, and where would she go if she did escape. There was no way of knowing which way her dad would be coming from even if she did make it to the main road. She meant what she had said to her father. The slick guy she had seen briefly was definitely running the show, and she didn't trust him.

Before she could think any more, she heard a scratching noise coming from the outside of the window. Muffled shouts came from outside just as the window rose and Lexie was greeted by the smiling face of Nigel, her father's assistant. Lexie ran to the window and allowed herself to be lifted out to the safe ground below. Her father stood just a few feet away, and she ran to him, throwing her arms around his neck. He ushered her away to a waiting car, once inside he hugged her again.

"I'm so sorry baby," he choked hoarsely, "Did they hurt you?"

"No, I was just scared. Is Nikki alright?"

"I believe so; I think you're going to like the other surprise I have for you too."

"What?"

"You'll see," he smiled, turning his attention to the approaching Doug with Scott Chambers limping along beside him. "I need to stay here, with the authorities, and that chick that was in there. Nigel get them back to the plane, I'll meet you guys back in Abbeville. I hear that game is tomorrow, I'd like to have some down time after this little adventure!"

Larson smiled, "Absolutely,"

Nigel moved to sit behind the wheel of the car. "You don't have to say it Sir, I know where we're going," There was a twinkle in his eye as he put the car in gear, pulling into the road past blaring police cars that were speeding along toward the cabin.

When Nigel stopped the car, Lexie looked at the expansive plane sitting idle on the runway. "Wow, that's big!" she said to her father.

"Yep, and your surprise is aboard, so let's go see shall we?"

There were moments in life that everyone experienced. Bittersweet moments that brought tears of joy to even the most staid person. Lexie climbed the stairs of the elegant Learjet and stepped aboard a few steps ahead of her father and his friends. In wonder she looked around and saw the woman stand nervously, tears streaming down her face. "Lexie?" she said, a look of wonder and relief encompassing her face. There was no question, not to Lexie, this woman before her was her mother. She ran to her, and hugged her, the long thought dreams of a teenager finally coming true. Her parents were at last together, and she had her mother back.

Larson stood back for a second, then joined his wife and daughter in the embrace. As he soothed the hair of his daughter with one hand, his other brushed the nape of Margo's neck, soothing, lovingly, complete.

Nigel coughed loudly to get their attention. "I think if we sit, we'll be able to take off and get home. What do you say Boss?"

Larson smiled at Nigel and nodded, reaching for Margo's hand. "Absolutely, let's go home!"

~~~~~

When Larson, Margo and Lexie walked into the warm interior of the Evans' living room, they were greeted with the usual haphazard din of family. Sylvia looked up into the smiling eyes of her oldest son and took in the sight beside him with grace and wonder. Margo held his hand, beside them Lexie beamed with delight. True wonders never ceased in their world she marveled. Her baby's family was whole again.

Everyone seemed to start talking at once. Nikki, hearing the commotion came in from the kitchen drying her hands on a towel. She saw her friend standing next to her brother, the glorious happy look of her niece beside her mother, and succumbed to the tears of joy that welled up inside her. She moved swiftly across the floor of the living room and threw her arms around her brother. "Now we're ready for Christmas, Big Brother," she said, hugging him.

"And we're going to have a nice long talk about secret keeping!" he said, tongue in cheek, because no matter what had happened in the past, his love was beside him now, and the past no longer mattered. The future, however, was a different story. He wasn't sure how he was going to meld all the pieces of his life but he knew one thing. There would never be a separation between him and Margo again.

Later that evening, in the room Larson had where Larson had spent most of his childhood, the reunited couple lay wrapped in each other's arms. Just down the hall in a spare bedroom between her grand-parents and parents rooms their daughter slept soundly.

After about a pot of coffee and a meal of cold cuts and pastries, Margo had disappeared outside. Larson had watched her, talking on her phone, and gave her the privacy she had needed. He wanted to know who she had been talking to, but didn't know if he should ask. They had not spoken of any decisions, but there were several to be made. Somewhere in his heart he knew he still had a job to do, but his daughter, their daughter, was finally happy. There had to be a way to combine both of their worlds.

Hating to break the silence, but knowing the answers had to be found, he tightened his hold on the sleepy woman in his arms.

"I think we need to talk," he said simply.

"I know we do. I don't want to rock the boat, and I'm afraid maybe I've assumed too much. But I wanted to reassure you that I've made a pretty big decision regardless."

Larson held his breath while she continued.

Margo lifted her hand searching for his, and laced her fingers with his. "I called Darcy. I turned the management of the shop over to her. She's been ready for a while, and I think it's time I stopped running away and came home. To you, if you'll have me."

In one fluid movement he switched their positions to cradle her in his arms, his blue eyes searching hers with intent and wonder.

"Are you sure?" Tenderly he touched her face, the lump of emotion nearly blocking his airflow.

She nodded, becoming more confident in her decision. "My place is with you now."

"And your grandfather?"

"I don't think anyone can interfere with your accomplishments. You are strong and successful, and you've made a name for yourself. The important thing is for us to stop wasting so much time."

Larson smiled and lowered his head, tenderly catching her lips with his own. "Then let's go home." He grinned and added, "After the football game of course."

~~~~~

There was a lot of screaming and cheering in front of the television the next afternoon. In amongst the happy family members, Sylvia surveyed her full living room with happiness. She watched her granddaughter, wearing her bright red Carolina Gamecocks jersey getting tickled and teased by her Dad who sported Clemson Orange with glee and mischievous laughter. Margo looked on lovingly at both of them smiling, her hand gently rubbing Larson's shoulder. They were going to have a great Christmas this year, no doubt.

She turned her attention to her daughter Nikki and smiled. Now there was a project that warranted time and energy. Sylvia smiled inwardly and went toward the kitchen for more supplies. Planning was going to be needed.

Epilogue

Two months later Margo was hosting a New Year's Day party in her home. She smiled as Lexie bounced around with her friends, playing a new game on her video game system. Larson stood next to a massive Christmas tree with a tall glass of iced tea in his hand. She touched his arm lovingly as she walked back towards the kitchen, a sleek smile on her face.

Since they had returned to Boston the charges against Scott had been dropped. He moved back to New Hampshire to live near his mother. Gail and Reggie were out of business and on their way to hard time. The bookstore that Margo had decided to open was almost ready for business; ironically the best spot she had found was in the lobby of Larson's building, next to the little coffee shop. It seemed everything was back to normal and they had everything.

Margo looked out into the back yard while she drained the celery for another party platter. The extremely elegant kitchen held a lot of quiet contemplation for her. The granite counters were smooth, cool and welcoming. She arranged the rinsed vegetables on the platter surrounding the homemade vegetable dip and called out to Larson.

"Do you want these now?"

She didn't know he had followed her into the kitchen and stood behind her. He slipped his arms around her and nuzzled her neck.

"You have to be a bit more specific, Darling," he growled wickedly, "I want a lot of things now. But we have guests on the way over here thanks to your new found love of entertaining."

Margo smiled and turned her head slightly, allowing him to capture her lips in a kiss that held promise of something yet to come.

The doorbell rang just then and the two separated just as Lexie had come into the kitchen to get a drink. "You two are starting to make that a habit... I feel like I'm in a soap opera."

Truth be told Lexie couldn't be happier that her parents had reconciled. Every teenage girls dream come true. She was mostly glad that she was able to put the gifts her mother had been sending out for display. All around her room were little mementos of her life. The quotes and notes were in her scrapbook except for the last one... which was on her mirror in her bathroom. She smiled and looked at her parents

again, and said, tongue in cheek, "You guys just relax,
I'll get the door."

She unscrewed the cap of the bottle of water
she had gotten and took a long sip before she opened
the door, expecting to see another of her friends, or
Doug standing there. Instead she gasped and took a
step back. There before her stood an elderly
gentleman, leaning heavily on a dark wooden cane.
His eyes glistened with tears as he stared at her.
"Alexis?" he whispered incredulously.

"Who is it--" Margo was saying when she came
behind her, but knew as soon as she saw the older
man. "Papa!" she took a step back in fear backing
into Larson who came to stand behind her.

The old man took in the sight before him. The
young man he had scorned tuned out to be a strong
man, protecting his family, loving unconditionally. He
was successful and capable and Senor Grenaldi had
been wrong. He could admit that, and held up his
hand in surrender.

"A moment of your time, then I'll go," he
pleaded, "if you want."

Margo stood to the side and let him in. He
didn't seem so out of place as he walked in to the

grand room. Nigel appeared beside the man and looked toward Larson for direction.

"Nigel, please take Senor Grenaldi's coat."

"Of course Sir," Larson gestured to the leather sofa in the room in front of the entertainment center. Margo watched as the man who had raised her lowered himself to the richly decorated sofa and smiled. "It's good to see you Papa. I'm glad you're here.

Robert Grenaldi looked up surprised. "Really Marguerite? After all this time, all this trouble I've caused with my short sightedness? I don't deserve that, but you," he leveled his eyes to Larson, "You I owe a debt I don't believe I can ever repay." He looked down at his lap, his hands joined together. "But I'm sorry. If there was anything I've learned in these years, it's this. I was wrong to make you leave him Marguerite. Them. Can you ever forgive me?"

Margo took in the sight of her grandfather, complacent and pleading and had no reserve. She lowered herself to kneel in front of him, her eyes shining with tears. "There's nothing to forgive Papa," she said, "I love you."

The old man broke then, tears of joy spilled down his cheeks, "I love you too, *Querida,* so much."

"Oh Papa," Margo sobbed, throwing her arms around his neck and holding him.

A while later, Robert was watching his grand-daughter dance to a video game on the screen of the large plasma television. His hand grasped the arm of the couch, a smile of contentment on his features. Margo brought out another plate of dip and appetizers and Robert looked at the plate before him in small wonder.

"You cooked this?"

Margo smiled, linking hands with Larson and nodded.

"Simply fascinating." Robert Grenaldi murmured, reaching for a canapé. He put the small morsel in his mouth and sighed, closing his eyes. "Delicious. You do this a lot? You like it?"

Margo laughed then, "Yes Papa, I love it."

"Fascinating."

Lexie looked over her shoulder as the song ended and smiled. More than she could ever have hoped for, all her dreams seemed to be coming true at last.

Larson joined hands with his wife and smiled at her. "Happy?" he murmured in her ear.

"You have no idea, but I'll show you later."

The End

Acknowledgements:

Without the help of some very important people this work of fiction would not be possible.

First and foremost: My Heavenly Father, and my Savior Jesus Christ, who lends me strength every day;

To my parents: Robert and Linda Wildes, for teaching me books are a window to the world;

To my Aunt Kathy Scott, owner of Sweet Expressions in Abbeville, South Carolina. She has let me shadow her many times to bring life to my fictional Evans family;

I also wish to thank my grandparents, Ms. Evelyn B Page, and the late Benjamin L Page, for providing such a vivid childhood, sharing their home in Abbeville with me nearly every summer;

I especially want to thank my editor
Cricket S. McDonnell. What a great gift you are
to my life. Here's to a long working
relationship.

Turn the page for a sneak peak at
"No Strings", the second book of "The
Festival Series"

Prologue

Almost 17 years ago.

In the band room of the high school, Nikki Evans and her fellow cast-mates were putting the finishing touches on their make-up. She smiled at her reflection while smoothing the stage make up base around her face, catching the gaze of her longtime friend Glenda McKinley.

"It's all a game, you know."

"What is?" the girl asked, fixing the grayish white wig atop her head, hiding the dark curls that usually hung in springy tendrils. It was one of her traits that Nikki most envied. Those dark curls on her own head would complete the pixie illusion she wanted so badly, but yet God had not graced her with such luxurious locks, but rather straight brown hair that had a tendency to fly away in unruly wisps if she cut it any shorter than her customary shoulder length hair.

Nikki was playing 'Marian', the librarian in the Abbeville High School Theater and Music

Department's production of 'The Music Man."
Glenda was playing her mother.

"Love, life, everything!" Nikki said, putting
the make-up brush back in its case with a flick.
Choosing an eye-liner, she leaned closer to the
mirror and continued talking.

"You hear these guys around us. 'So and
so didn't get invited to a party,' 'Nobody wants to
go to prom because the song is wrong.' It's all a
game...If you keep this thought in mind it will
never catch you off guard. It's all a game!"

"Sounds jaded to me," Glenda said, patting
the string of pearls she'd be wearing for their first
scene.

"You'll see," Nikki said, closing her make
up case and standing to smooth the skirt of her
costume. "I plan to never take anything so
seriously. I'm going places. A lot further than
Abbeville, South Carolina, I promise you!"

"You have a great voice," Glenda agreed
encouragingly.

"I have a great attitude," Nikki corrected.
"I'm not going to get stuck married like my brother

Larson seems to want, or alone for ever like Adriana swears she'll be. No, I'm going to be happy, and always in control of myself."

The Stage Manager, James Harvey tapped on the door to the band-room and yelled over the din of giggles and squeals. "Five minutes ladies...I need chorus girls lined up front and center now!! Nikki...you lead the rest of them out please...you ready?"

"Born ready!" Nikki said triumphantly walking to the center of the room.

The other girls joined her forming a circle. They all grasped hands and held for a moment, then Nikki counted, "3....2....1...." and they all yelled, "Let's do this!"

Several girls of the chorus scampered out with Nikki following, giving her friend a thumbs up sign.

Glenda smiled to herself and looked at Ms. Manville, their advisor, and the producer of the show.

"That girl is going to get knocked on her butt!" she said to the teacher.

"By who?" Ms. Manville asked, raising her eyebrows.

"Not who, what." Glenda laughed, nudging their advisor. "Real love, of course. It will happen someday, and when it does...she won't know what hit her!"

15423621R00104

Made in the USA
Charleston, SC
02 November 2012